Praise for LINGER AW
from the British press

An adult fairy tale, an outrageous and genial fantasy of love, sex and death ... a unique and peculiar union of the every day and the wholly surreal. Nobody can mix the philosophical with the downright cheesy like he can. — *The Independent*

Burst(s) with energy, invention, wit, observation and just plain oddity. — *The Guardian*

Linger Awhile, the blessed 14th novel by Russell Hoban who. . . . remains by far the most imaginative novelist in Britain. The writing throughout is by turns hilariously owlish and magisterially concise — often both. The primary pleasure of this book, and of Hoban's writing in general, is the unsullied joy at the strange great coincidence of life that breathes through every sentence. — *Independent on Sunday*

Russell Hoban is the most intimate of geniuses. . . he is the author of novels that use the quotidian as a springboard for ever more extravagant leaps into the unknown. His unique, oblique, animistic viewpoint on love and the world has won him critical panegyrics and legions of devoted fans, but he remains a word-of-mouth writer.

— *Independent on Sunday* interview with Mr. Hoban

Praise for Russell Hoban's work

Russell Hoban's perfectly cadenced, slyly comic prose is ambrosia. — *Washington Post Book World*

Russell Hoban has proven himself a wordsmith and a punster on a par with Lewis Carroll and James Joyce.

— *New York Newsday*

Russell Hoban is our ur-novelist, a maverick voice that is like no other. He can take themes that seem too devastating for contemplation and turn them into allegories in which wry, sad humor is married to quite extraordinary powers of imagery and linguistic fertility that makes each book a linguistic departure. — *Sunday Telegraph*

Russell Hoban is an original, imaginative and inventive. Though some of his work has been compared with that of Tolkein or C. S. Lewis, he is his own man, working his own vein of magical fantasy. — *The Times* (London)

I've often thought of Russell Hoban as a sentimental Samuel Beckett for people who would rather Vladimir and Estragon just did something while waiting for Godot not to show up. — *Sunday Telegraph*

Hoban is the best sort of genius. Far too interesting to be shortlisted for major prizes, far too dynamic to be condemned as a national treasure, he seems to write books for the sole purpose of making sense of life, while never being too bothered that it rarely does. — *The Guardian*

Linger Awhile

Russell Hoban

LINGER AWHILE

DAVID R. GODINE · *Publisher*

BOSTON

To Jüri and Lynette

First published in 2007 by
DAVID R. GODINE · *Publisher*
Post Office Box 450
Jaffrey, New Hampshire 03452
www.godine.com

Originally published in Great Britain by
Bloomsbury Publishing Plc, 2006

Design, composition & toad ornament by Carl W. Scarbrough

LIBRARY OF CONGRESS CATALOGING-IN-PUBLICATION DATA

Hoban, Russell.
Linger awhile / Russell Hoban.
  p. cm.
ISBN-13: 978-1-56792-326-1
ISBN-10: 1-56792-326-7
1. Older men—Fiction. 2. Cowgirls—Fiction. 3. Virtual reality—
Fiction. I. Title.
PS3558.O336L48   2007
813'.54—dc22
2007000123

FIRST U.S. EDITION
Printed in Canada

I've something to tell you, so linger awhile.

Contents

1 🐖 Irving Goodman

13 NOVEMBER 2003. I fell in love with Charlotte Burton the first time I heard her voice, months before I actually met her. This was back in 1966 when she was at Radio Essex, Britain's Better Music Station on Knock John in the Thames Estuary. Her voice had an elegant eroticism that was effortless; that it came to me via pirate radio gave it the added charm of the forbidden. I bought the nautical chart of the estuary and reveled in its esoterica. The unseen Charlotte became for me a princess hedged about with buoys and soundings and magical names. Knock John Tower, the old World War II fort where she worked, was shown, with the eponymous sandbank and channel as well as Barrow, Long Sand, Fisherman's Gat Precautionary Area, and other names that sang in my mind while my fantasies rose and fell with the tides.

When I finally met Charlotte she was exactly as she sounded and from the first moment everything was as I hoped it would be. We were married and had ten good years together. We were faithful to each other and I had no mid-life crisis. Then she died. Nobody talks about end-of-life crises but they do happen and twenty-seven years after Charlotte's death I fell into one at the age of eighty-three. I needed some technical help with it so I bought a bottle of expensive whiskey and went to see Istvan Fallok at Hermes Soundways in Soho.

I handed him the bottle and he read the label. "Bowmore Cask Strength Islay Single Malt Scotch Whisky. Thank you, I'm deeply moved." He found two cloudy glasses somewhere; maybe he washed them every six months, I don't know. He poured for us both and I added water from a kettle that was sitting on some sheet music. He tried his neat. "Here's to whatever," he said, and swallowed a little. Then he coughed, blew out a big breath, wiped his eyes, added water, and said, "This must be serious."

"It is," I said. We were in the deep-sea grotto of his basement sound studio off Broadwick Street. November rain was pinging on the steel stairs that led down to his door. Little red and yellow and green eyes winked while a humming silence listened. Dim shapes crouched and towered and unheard decibels rose and fell in blue columns on screens.

"Don't be bashful," he said. "Blurt it out."

"OK," I blurted. "I'm in love."'

"Mazel tov. What're you now, ninety-five?" He was only in his early sixties.

"Eighty-three."

"You look older. Still get it up?"

"Don't be coarse. 'Love is not love / Which alters where it alteration finds.'"

"So it's all in your mind then."

"So are you, so is everything. I experience the world through my cerebral cortex."

"Please, no fancy talk. What's her name?"

"Justine Trimble."

"And she's what, twenty-five?"

"She was. Now she's dead."

"Great. You're old and she's dead. So what do you want from me?"

"Get me to her. Or her to me, I don't care which."

"You want to go to her, no problem: slash your wrists, throw yourself under a train, whatever."

"Come on, you know what I mean."

"No, I don't. If you're going to have a mid-life crisis at the age of eighty-three at least do it with a woman who's available. Who is this Justine Trimble anyhow?"

"Here, look at this." I'd brought a video with me, *Last Stage to El Paso.* The Internet Movie Database showed that she'd been in fourteen films but there were only four on commercial videotape and I had them all. I stuck it in the machine and we watched it. Justine Trimble was pretty in a 1950s black-and-white western kind of way but she was more than just pretty – she had something about her that made me fall in love with her the first time I saw her swing into the saddle. In several of her films she co-starred with Dawson Chase, a much bigger star than she was. Westerns back then had not yet achieved political correctness. Justine Trimble had what it took for the time. You could tie her to a post and leave her out in the rain for two or three days and she'd come out of it freshly laundered, make-up unsmudged, and with dry knickers. When the action required it, she loaded guns, bandaged wounds (nobody bled but they would hold themselves where they were shot) and she said, "Look out, here they come," as necessary. In *Last Stage to El Paso* they actually let her rescue Dawson Chase. She had an exemplary figure, a modestly unassailable bosom, and was an expert horsewoman much admired for her seat. When she and Dawson kissed they didn't use their tongues and when they embraced he kept his hands above her waist. She was wasted on him. Why did I love her? Why not someone my own age from a similar background? I have nothing against eighty-three-year-old women but love isn't rational, it isn't correct. It can strike like lightning anywhere, any time. Wham, that's it. The first time I saw her I knew she was the one I'd been waiting for through my years of loneliness.

Fallok was watching the film attentively. In the scene where Justine goes after the bad guys she was wearing what would have been jeans if they'd been made by Levi Strauss but these had been run up by the wardrobe department and although lycra hadn't yet been invented they brought out the best in Justine. As she swung into the saddle Fallok backed up the tape, then made her swing into the saddle again. "Why'd you do that?" I said.

"Just checking something."

"Checking her ass, you mean."

"Oh, and I suppose you fell in love with her mind?" He behaved himself for the rest of the film. Dawson saved the gold shipment, Justine saved Dawson, they kissed with closed mouths and it was THE END.

"OK," said Fallok, "now I know who she is. Was. What am I expected to do about it?"

"I *told* you – get me to her or her to me."

"What *her*? You've got her on video and the real Justine is an ex-her. What her are you talking about?"

"Don't play dumb – I want the whole flesh-and-blood Justine in 3-D where I can get my hands on her."

"Where is this 3-D Justine supposed to come from?"

"From the video. She's in there in the form of magnetized particles or whatever. In those particles you must be able to find her visual DNA."

"Visual DNA! Did you read this or are you making it up as you go along?"

"It just came out of my mouth. Is there such a thing?"

"I don't know. I've never done anything with image enhancement or reconstruction. I'm not the man for the job."

"Sure you are, you can do anything with technology. I know you can do it." He was smart and he was weird and that made me believe in him.

He didn't say anything for a bit and I could see that he was mentally replaying Justine as she swung into the saddle. Then, "Let me think about this for a couple of weeks."

"Try to think fast. I haven't been feeling all that well and I might be checking out pretty soon."

"Leave the video and I'll see what I can do. Mind you, I can't promise anything and I might have to damage the tape."

"That's OK, I've got a copy. I know you'll figure something out. When can I call you?"

"Don't call me, I'll call you when I have anything to report."

14 November 2003. It was Herman Orff who put me on to Istvan Fallok. Orff was in his sixties by then. He and Fallok were both famous among the people I knew, writers, painters, composers, and various others on the way up or the way down or treading water in the arts. Between fifteen and twenty years ago Orff, who got very small advances and whose books never earned back those advances, was suffering from what we in the trade call blighter's rock. He was totally rocked and couldn't get anything useful down on paper. While in that state he received a handbill through his letterbox in which Istvan Fallok claimed that he could unrock anyone. The rest (among a rather small circle) is history.

By means of thirty-six electrodes and who knows what computerized mumbo-jumbo, Orff had his head zapped by Fallok and had a number of encounters with the head of Orpheus. Eventually he found his way into cereal boxes, the backs of, and eked out a living in that medium while developing a character called Nnvsnu the Tsrungh which he copyrighted as a computer game that made him almost wealthy.

Orff was white-haired and rosy-faced, and he was what you might call a successful failure. He had failed as a novelist, and he had failed to regain his lost love, Luise von Himmelbett, (see his novel, *The Medusa Frequency*) but he could smile (ruefully) and say that really he had no complaints. "Life is a one-way trip," he said to me. "If someone nice sits next to you for a while, that's as much as you have a right to expect." It was at a publisher's party that he told me this, the occasion being the launch of Geoffrey Thrust's novel, *Love's Labia*, at the Horse Hospital behind Russell Square tube station. Neither of us knew Thrust but we were on the Palinurus mailing list.

"Do you think Istvan Fallok could do anything with a visual problem?" I said. Having drunk more red wine than I should have I outlined my situation at length.

"Fallok can do all kinds of things," said Orff. "Try him and see. The worst that can happen is that it will cost you your sanity and maybe your life but you'll probably be sorry if you don't ring him up."

Who could say no to a proposition like that? Orff gave me Fallok's number and I rang him up. When I met him I was impressed by his appearance. How a man could look so worn-out without being dead was a real head-shaker. I'm told that his hair used to be red but it was white now. His face hung loosely from his watery blue eyes but he looked sharp in an almost extinct way and this was the man to whom I confided my cask strength whiskey and my hopes.

13 DECEMBER 2003. I tried to be patient. I fully appreciated that I'd asked Fallok to do something that, as far as I knew, had never been done and very likely *couldn't* be done. When I was a child we had a large mirror that took up most of the width of the rear wall in the front room. It had no frame and was fastened flush against the wall. It showed what was in front of it but I used to put my face against the very edge and try to see around it to what it wasn't showing. I never could but I knew that the mirror wasn't giving me the whole picture. I'm still trying to see around the edge. That's where Justine was and I believed that Istvan Fallok could get me there.

I waited a week, then a month. I watched my copy of *Last Stage to El Paso* again and again, straining my eyes in an effort to pull her out of the screen and out of death into my world.

My eyesight was failing. Age-related macular degeneration was the diagnosis. The macula is that part of the eye which gives detail and depth perception. I frequently mistook flat surfaces for raised ones and shadows for substance. I always drank most of a bottle of red wine at dinner and that didn't help. In the evening it was difficult for me to read with my reading glasses and images on the TV screen lost sharpness. In a surprising number of films there's a bit where someone holds up a letter and I couldn't read it unless I got up very close. If it was a video I could pause the tape but if it wasn't I often missed crucial information. Sometimes people killed themselves or someone else after reading a letter.

I was having difficulty with color too; the scene before my eyes sometimes seemed pale. It wasn't cataracts – I'd already had implants for those. Dr. Luzhin is my eye doctor. He looks like Lenin and strokes his goatee a lot. When I asked him about the color problem he put drops in my eyes, sent me back to the waiting room for fifteen minutes, then led me to the apparatus where you put your chin on the chin rest, shone lights of various colors into one eye and the other, and stroked his goatee. "What?" I said.

"There's no change in your eyes since six months ago," he said. "This business with loss of color, there is no defense against it. What you see is what the brain tells you you're seeing. If the brain decides that the color is going out of the world, you're going to see everything paler than before."

"Is there anything I can do about it?"

"Get yourself a girlfriend."

I waited and waited for word from Istvan but there was no news day after day. Then I began to see Justine Trimble where she wasn't. If I looked out of the corner of my eye I saw her in the street, in the Underground, and on buses in black-and-white. She always looked back at me as if she wanted to say something. When I looked straight ahead she wasn't there.

2 🐗 Istvan Fallok

24 NOVEMBER 2003. "They all laughed at Wilbur and his brother. When they said that man could fly..." Right? General disbelief. But the Wright brothers suspended their disbelief. They believed that man *could* fly and the rest of it followed from that. Suspension of disbelief is the first step in doing anything hitherto thought impossible. Yes. I keep telling myself that. I'm Istvan Fallok and I believe that I'm going to reconstitute Justine Trimble from the magnetized particles of a videotape. I believe it because when I saw her on that video it hit me like a bolt of lightning. Wham, I was in love. Irving Goodman's an OK guy and he's in love with Justine too but if I can make this happen she's going to be mine, not his.

Right, let's get practical. Google tells me that videotape is composed primarily of three components: magnetic (metal oxide) particles, a polyurethane-based binder, and a polyester base material. Particles yes. Particles and waves. Diffraction gratings. Particles in suspension. Particles in a suspension of disbelief. Waves of aggravation and frustration. Light comes through the grating as waves or particles. Interference patterns. Light. Justine on the video is made of light.

Wait a minute. Let's think this thing through. Do I want to bring Justine to me or do I want to go to her? Not dead Justine but the waves and or particles of her on the video? So if I go there, what then? Will I be the sixty-five-year-old me or will I be young like Justine? And western? With a pistol and a horse?

There was a name in my mind: Gösta Kraken. I had a copy

of his book, *Perception Perceived.* I went to my shelves, stuck out my arm, and it leapt into my hand. So I knew it wanted to help. I'd flagged the page where he talks about being:

Being is not a steady state but an occulting one: we are all of us a succession of stillnesses blurring into motion on the wheel of action, and it is in those spaces of black between the pictures that we find the heart of the mystery in which we are never allowed to rest. The flickering of a film interrupts the intolerable continuity of apparent world; subliminally it gives us those in-between spaces of black that we crave. The eye is hungry for this; eagerly it collaborates with the unwinding strip of celluloid that shows it twenty-four stillnesses per second, making real by an act of retinal retention the here-and-gone, the continual disappearing in which the lovers kiss, the shots are fired, the horses gallop; but below the threshold of conscious thought the eye sees and the mind savors the flickering of the black.

Thank you, Gösta. So it's light and motion, blackness and stillness. Waves or particles? Waves *and* particles? Still, I'm thinking of it from her end. What about my getting to where *she* is? No good. Even if I could work out the translation of me into magnetized particles, all I'd have is me stuck in *Last Stage to El Paso.* Endlessly. No, I've got to bring her to me. First I'll have to scan the stillnesses and calibrate an electronic suspension of the black. Film runs at twenty-four frames per second; video at twenty-five and the black... Hang on, do I want the black? No, I don't. Let's back up and start again.

25.11.03. Sorry, Gösta. Can't use you this time but maybe some other time. We're talking about light here, not blackness. Jus-

9

tine on screen is particles of light. Or waves, whichever. OK, so I've got to get a frame with a good full-length shot of Justine, then I isolate her for transmission. How the fuck do I do that?

Went to see Chauncey Lim in D'Arblay Street. Optical novelties. All kinds of pocket-size things with lenses, keyrings that talk and buttonhole cameras. On the wall an acupuncture chart and a calendar with a photograph of a black rooster from Aunt Zophrania's Herbals & Dreambooks Est. 1925 "Harlem's Best". The place was pretty fuggy and there was the kind of smell you might get if you opened a box of Transylvanian earth. You have to take Chauncey as you find him. I bought a fountain pen that projects a photo of Virginia Mayo (still big in Morocco) to put him in a good mood.

"You already have three of these," he said. "What do you want from me this time?"

I said, "I'm almost afraid to tell you, it's such a crazy idea."

He began to look interested. "Crazy is good," he said. "Too much not enough crazy in this world. Tell me anything, I'm very electric."

"You mean eclectic."

"That too, but I sing the body electric. I'm talking Walt Whitman here."

"Please don't. Can I tell you what I want now?"

"OK. Always you're in a hurry, Istvan. Slow down, smell the flowers, listen to the birds."

"There aren't any birds, the radiators are knocking and what I smell isn't flowers."

"It's High John the Conqueror root, I grind it up and make little incense cones out of it. This root gives power, it's good luck, one of Aunt Zophrania's top sellers."

"Right, are you going to let me tell you my problem now?"

"Go ahead. I can see that your problem wants to become my problem."

So I told him and he became quite excited. "This is top crazy," he said. "Show me the video."

I handed him *Last Stage to El Paso*. He put it in his VCR and played it, backing it up now and then to see a scene again. "This is a woman I could fall in love with," he said.

"First of all, she's dead," I said.

"Nobody's perfect," he said.

"And I saw her first," I said.

"Keep your shirt on. You want to isolate her, this is what you have to do." He gave me detailed instructions and I took notes.

"Let me know what happens," Chauncey said as I was leaving.

"You bet," I said.

"Here," he said, "take some High John with you, you'll want all the power you can get." He gave me a box of the little incense cones.

"Thanks," I said. "See you." I hurried home and got started while everything was still fresh in my mind. With Chauncey's instructions I converted the video to a digitized version that I could scan frame by frame. I got a JPEG of the frame I wanted, then I started up Photoshop and highlighted the background. I went to the inverse of that and got Justine with black all around her which I cut out and pasted on a blank Photoshop canvas. So far, so good.

What I had in mind was to do a small-size trial run first. In order to use a diffraction grating I devised a converter that would laserize the light from the Justine figure and aim it at the slits in the diffraction grating. The grating was something I remembered from sixth-form physics. This was a low-tech job made of cardboard and only fourteen inches high with two slits in it. I had a sheet of photographic printing paper covered with foil on a little easel about two feet away. I darkened the room, put Justine up on the screen, triggered the laser, and uncovered the paper as the interference pattern appeared. Then I covered it again, went into the darkroom, and printed it. That gave me the particles of the interference pattern on the paper. I dissolved the paper in hydrochloric acid and then what I had on the bottom of the tray were the particles alone.

1 JANUARY 2004. Everything grinds to a halt for Christmas but I took a taxi out to Thierson & Bates Biologicals in Surrey and got some frog specimens before they closed. Chauncey Lim helped me out with the chemicals I needed and by New Year's Eve I was ready to have a go.

I poured the particles into a test tube containing polypeptides that I'd prepared from the frogs. I figured that my primordial soup would bind the particles in a suspension of disbelief and the frog DNA wouldn't interfere with the identity of the particles. I lit the High John cones and when the room smelled lucky I zapped the soup with 240 volts. Smoke came out of the test tube and there was an electrical smell. Then Jesus Christ, there she was in the test tube in black-and-white, about four inches high. She looked scared, and stood there twisting slowly with her arms above her head because of the narrowness of the tube. As I looked at her from all angles I had a crazed feeling of power. Then I suddenly felt so sad that I began to cry. I was shaking, and with the test tube in my left hand I put my right hand behind me so I could lean on the table but I pricked my finger on the point of a scalpel. When I held up my hand a drop of blood fell into the test tube and all at once tiny Justine blossomed into color. She looked at me and mouthed, 'Oh!' Then the color faded and with it the whole figure, ghastly in monochrome as it shriveled into nothing. Oh, my God, the sadness! I stood there holding the test tube and looking at the emptiness where she'd been with my head spinning round on the first day of the New Year.

3 ⬤ Irving Goodman

2 JANUARY 2004. Finding and losing! I found Justine in the lonely night-time hours when I watched westerns and drank myself to sleep. Men quick to anger, loyal unto death, fast on the draw. Horses beautiful and innocent. Women to inspire a good man and madden a bad one. Mountains and plains and rivers, canyons, arroyos, gulches and draws. Mists of morning and moons over the desert. Justine flickering in my sodden half-dreams and my forlorn hopes.

Having found her, was I now to lose her to Istvan Fallok? Was this ordained, written in the Big Book of Absurdity? I had turned to Fallok to make Justine real for me and now I knew in my heart that he was out to take her from me. The way he leered when she swung into the saddle, Oh God. Has he brought her into our reality or has he gone into hers? Wherever they are, I'll find them and take her away from him, that bastard. Him and his high-tech treachery. Don't go with him, Justine, I saw you first.

4 🐿 Chauncey Lim

3 JANUARY 2004. Justine Trimble. There is that about her which moves me deeply and stirs profoundly the essential Chauncey, the inner Lim. Istvan Fallok, that creep. Every now and then he comes round and buys a Virginia Mayo pen and expects me to do anything he requires of me. Insufferable cheek. The white man patronizing the yellow brother. Why then do I do that which he asks me to do? Do I need his goodwill? No, I piss on his goodwill.

Justine Trimble. The very thought of her makes my heart sing. Fallok is all wrong for her and I intend to make her mine. This is the first time I've put it into words but there it is. Where is he or where are they now? He said he would let me know what's happening but I've heard nothing. Which means that something *is* happening. Otherwise he'd have come round to buy another pen.

I went to Elijah's Lucky Dragon, Rosalie Chun's restaurant in Golders Green. Rosalie's maiden name was Cohen but she married into North Chinese cuisine, wears iridescent cheongsams although she's fourteen stone, and has mingled Golders Green with North China to the point where she is now to cholesterol what Charlton Heston is to rifles. I had latkes Xingjiang with sour cream. While I was doing quality belching and drinking jasmine tea Rosalie came over to my table. "Hi Chaunce," she said. "How're they hanging?"

"Uncertainly," I said. "Yourself?"

"A day older than yesterday but not much wiser. You look troubled."

"I am," I said. "Profoundly."

"Woman?"

"Yes, but it's probably an impossible love."

"The best kind," she said. "Don't move – I'll bring you chicken soup Lucky Dragon with industrial-strength matzah balls. This will put roses in your cheeks and yang in your schlong, guaranteed."

"Matzah balls?" I said.

"With Yongzheng ingredients," she said. "Very secret, don't ask."

I partook of the soup and I felt that my probably impossible love might be negotiable. I said to Rosalie, "I am now spiritually refreshed and ready for whatever comes next. Thank you."

"What are friends for?" she said. "And remember, in the immortal words of Rabbi Whatshisname from Kotzk, 'If you can't get over it, get under it.'"

"I'll remember that," I said. What I did next was go down to Istvan Fallok's place for a butcher's at the mad genius. I didn't go in but through the glass I could see him sitting with his head in his hands. There were various contraptions on his work table but no sign of Justine Trimble. So apparently no result yet.

5 🐻 Istvan Fallok

5 JANUARY 2004. Now what? Do I even want to think about it? The idea of it puts me off with its perversity and at the same time it turns me on. I can't get it off my mind, how the color went out of her and she shriveled up and became dust. That was just a little tiny Justine. With a full-size one it's a whole new ball game. And if I do it, where do we go from there?

6 🐿 Irving Goodman

6 JANUARY 2004. Almost two months and still no word from that treacherous bastard. Some people can't be trusted and inevitably they find idiots who trust them. I've always been stupid that way from childhood onward. When I swapped with other kids I always got the worst of the bargain. And was the victim of choice for bullies as well. "Four-Eyes", they called me, and knocked off my glasses. That's part of it – Fallok wouldn't try it on with someone who wouldn't stand for it. He thinks I can't do anything to stop him but we'll see about that.

I started hanging around his place to keep an eye on his comings and goings or his lying low, whichever. The blind was down so you couldn't see into the studio. There was a note on the door with a phone number. I called the number and a husky female voice said, "Hello."

"Who's this?" I said.

"Who wants to know?"

"Irv Goodman, I'm a friend of Istvan's. And you?"

"Grace Kowalski. He said you might call."

"Where is he?"

"He's away."

"Where?"

"I don't know. He didn't say."

"When's he coming back?"

"Didn't say. You know Istvan – when he doesn't *want* to say, he doesn't say."

"Where is this number that I'm talking to now?" I said.

"It's my shop, All That Glisters."

"Where's that?"

"In Berwick Street, towards the Oxford Street end, I'm

17

between Black Dog Music and the Raj Tandoori Restaurant."
She gave me the number.

"Can I come round to see you?"

"If you like. I can't tell you any more than I've already done
but maybe you can tell *me* something."

She sounded like vodka rather than scotch so on my way I
bought a bottle of Stolichnaya at Nicolas in Berwick Street and
proceeded to All That Glisters. Berwick Street was still busy
with foot traffic, cars, taxis, foodsy smells and people with
guidebooks looking in restaurant windows. Grace Kowalski's
shop was closed by now. Expensive-looking jewelry, strange
designs in the window behind the grating. Lights upstairs.
I rang the bell and she came down carrying a baseball bat. Tall
woman, gaunt, in her sixties I thought, gray hair in two long
plaits, denim shirt not tucked in, jeans, bare feet. Her feet
looked open-minded. "Hi," she said. We shook hands and I followed her upstairs to the flat, which was partly studio with a
workbench and a lot of tools and clutter. Various craftsman-
like smells: metal, soldering flux, blowtorch etc. She leaned the
bat in a corner. "Why the Louisville Slugger?" I said.

"I always carry a bat on the first date," she said.

"I always carry a bottle," I said, and gave her the Stolichnaya.

"Thank you," she said. "How did you know I liked vodka?"

"You sounded like vodka. In the nicest possible way."

"I'll take that as a compliment." She got two glasses. "Tonic
with it?" she said. "Ice?"

"Just as it comes," I said.

"My kind of drinker," she said, and poured.

"Here's looking at you," I said.

"And here's looking right back." We clank and drank.
"What's this all about?" she said. "Do you know?"

"I don't know where Istvan is, if that's what you mean.
You said you didn't either, but do you?"

"No," she said, "I wasn't lying. I haven't a clue."

"Istvan hasn't told you about Justine Trimble?"

"No, who's she?"

I told her everything I knew and my suspicions as well. Grace shook her head. "That bastard," she said. She tilted her head to one side and studied me for a few moments. "You're the kind of guy who gets pushed around, aren't you?"

I nodded.

"Me too," she said.

"You and Istvan...?"

"You could say we had some kind of understanding. Or rather, that's what I understood but maybe he didn't." She'd been pouring steadily and drinking a good deal faster than I. "Sometimes all you can do is make the best of a bad sitsatuation," she said. "Sisuashion. You know what I mean."

"Absolutely. As the *I Ching* says, 'When the river dries up, the superior woman drinks vodka.'"

"I'm drunk. Would you like to take advantage of me?"

"Very much. I regret that I am no longer a player."

"Don't regret. There's more than one way to skin a cat and you look like an imaginative guy." She lifted her shirt tails and dropped her jeans.

"If you put it that way," I said, and got imaginative.

In the morning we both woke up with no way to hold our heads that didn't hurt and we had coffee while considering what would come next. "Are you going to do anything about Istvan?" said Grace.

"So far," I said, "I've got nothing to go on but his absence and my suspicions."

"Which are probably correct."

"Have you got keys to his place?"

"Yes."

"Have you been inside since he left that message on the door?"

"Yes."

"And. . . ?"

"Come with me and see for yourself."

We went round to Fallok's place and down the steps to his grotto. Inside were a rank and earthy smell and various devices that I hadn't seen before. Conspicuous among them was an oil drum half full of what smelt like some primordial soup. Close by was a cardboard panel about six feet high with two slits side by side half-way up. I recognized it from high-school experiments as a diffraction grating. There were wings that could be folded to support it in an upright position. I stood it up and switched on what looked like a special kind of projector. On the cardboard Justine appeared in a still from *Last Stage to El Paso*. Beyond the diffraction grating on a white board was the interference pattern.

"What do you think?" I said to Grace.

She said, "I don't like the way that thing is looking at me with its two slitty eyes."

"OK, but apart from that?"

"I think he left all this in place because he wants us to see what he's doing."

"Which is?"

"What you told me: reconstituting Justine."

"And you believe he wants us to know about that?"

"Istvan's a funny guy. Maybe he's afraid of what he's got into and doesn't want to lose touch with the straight world." She was clinging to my arm. "Do you think he's done it? Reconstituted Justine Trimble?"

"If he found that he could, he certainly would."

"Why do the two of you have the hots for this twenty-five-year-old dead woman?"

"A dirty old man is the only kind of old man there is, Grace, and age brings out all kinds of strangeness."

"I don't mind strange. Would you stay with me tonight?"

"Sure, but let's go to my place. I want to check my e-mail and set the video timer."

"What are you going to record?"

"Bring Me the Head of Alfredo Garcia."

"Has it got a happy ending?"

"Not in the usual sense."

"I like happy endings."

"I have two machines. We can watch *Dead Letter Office* on the other one. That has a happy ending."

We were heading for Oxford Circus when I saw Istvan Fallok coming towards us in Marshall Street with someone on his arm – a woman I assumed. She was wearing a blue anorak with the hood up, tight gray jeans, and black-and-white cowboy boots. "Cowboy boots," I said. "Black-and-white." Balaclava and dark glasses under the hood. And gloves. When they saw us they stopped.

"Wotcher, Istvan?" I said. "What do you hear from El Paso?"

"I hear that the last stage left a while ago," he said. "Now, if you don't mind, there are times when four's a crowd."

"And two is one too many," said Grace. "But at least you could introduce us to your friend."

"Not just now," said Istvan. "We'll see you around."

"Maybe in Technicolor next time," I said as he and his silent companion walked past us and away.

7 🐸 Grace Kowalski

8 JANUARY 2004. So that was Miss Justine (Dead Meat) Trimble? Irv says Istvan bundled her up like that because she was only black-and-white. Maybe he'll unveil the full-color version at a later date. OK. If that's Istvan's idea of a really good time I wish him joy of it. Don't get me wrong, I have nothing against kinky. Kinky is OK in my book. Still, I suppose everyone draws the line somewhere. If I had a sister, would I want her to marry a necrophile? Consenting adults and all that. A prenuptial agreement with a posthumous clause. But then again.

Well, of course Irv is no better than Istvan really. He wants to get his hands on that dead meat too. Men are trouble enough when they're young, but when they're old! If I didn't know that form and emptiness are the same thing I'd be worried.

8 🐖 Chauncey Lim

8 JANUARY 2004. Obviously I wasn't going to hear from Istvan in the usual way so I made my preparations. I went to his place and I couldn't see in because the blinds were closed. I'd rigged a bug with a tiny radio mike and a buttonhole vidcam. The letterbox wasn't sealed so I stuck chewing gum on a non-vital part of the bug and put it in a little catapult meant for launching a toy helicopter. I stuck my hand through the letterbox, launched the bug, and hoped for the best. Then I went home to check the monitor.

The bug had stuck to the ceiling but not in a place that gave me much of a view. I got the top of a speaker or whatever and below that what I assumed was a female and very shapely leg ending in a black-and-white cowboy boot. I did better with the audio. I'll call the voices *I* and *J*:

I: Try to keep still, OK?

J: Why should I keep still? I didn't ask to come here, I'd rather be dead. What gives you the right to stick that thing in me?

I: I love you, that's what gives me the right.

J: That's what *you* think, you dried-up old piece of shit. Ow! That hurt.

I: If you'd hold still I could find the right place. Of course it's going to hurt if I keep getting it wrong. Ah, there we go. How's that?

J: Am I supposed to like it?

I: You've got a little color now and you're looking much better.

J: Get your hands off me, you creep. Stop taking my clothes off.

I: You're getting color from the top down, very nice. Ow! Why'd you hit me?

J: Just because you brought me back from the dead, don't think you can put your hands all over me.

I: Would you rather be dead?

J: Oh, never mind – you might as well finish now that you've started. If you've got enough of what it takes.

I: I feel a little faint but it's worth it to see you looking so good. Mmmmm!

J: Stop that! And what's going to happen when you're all used up?

I: We'll cross that bridge when we come to it.

J: What's that thing on the ceiling? It wasn't there before. Are you taking pictures of me?

(At this point Fallok removed the bug and stamped heavily on it.)

Her voice! Listening to them almost drove me mad. The pictures in my mind as I imagined what was going on! The erection it gave me! I took time out to pleasure myself but I still couldn't calm down, I was burning with passion, aching to possess this woman. My love had sprung up like a monstrous cactus the first time I saw her on video. Now Fallok is enjoying the fruits of my labor. I never should have told him how to go about it and I fully intend to take her away from him. Yes! To have her for myself, to feel her responding to the urgent life in me! One way or another I'll do it. Ah, Justine!

9 ⬛ Justine Trimble

8 JANUARY 2004. Crazy! Is this how Lazarus felt? And crazier from one minute to the next. I kept trying to push this old guy away but as the new life flowed into me I was getting horny. So I stopped pushing him away and pulled him on to me. If fucking was music he wouldn't of been no more than a tin whistle but in my mind it was Gene Autry giving it to me real good and singing, "Whoopee ti-yi-yo, rockin' to and fro, back in the saddle again..."

The old guy fainted when he finished and I must have used up too much juice because I could feel myself fading to black-and-white again which was a real comedown. When he opened his eyes the old guy – Istvan Fallok his name is – said, "How was it for you?"

"Terrific," I said. "Only I think I'm fading back to where I was at the beginning."

"I noticed," he said. "But I don't think I've got enough blood left to give you a top-up."

"So what's going to happen now?"

"You're a good-looking girl, Justine..."

"Yeah, so?"

"You could have guys queuing up for you."

"What, you're going to pimp for me?"

"Calm down, you don't have to go all the way – just get them in here and I'll soon have you in Technicolor again."

"When I get them in here you're going to do that business with the needles and tubes?"

"Unless you prefer the classical method of satisfying your need."

"You mean...?"

"Think Bela Lugosi, think children of the night."

"Jesus, you're trying to turn me into a vampire whore! I'm not some tramp you picked up, I was a *star*, I rode after the El Paso stage and saved the goddam gold."

"Justine, you don't like black-and-white much, it makes you feel terrible and you look like hell. I *told* you, just get the guys in here and I'll do all the heavy work."

"Never mind, I'll do it the old-fashioned way. I'll be a vampire whore. Come to think of it, I won't need you then, will I." I wanted to hit the street before my color was all gone, so I grabbed a jacket and headed for the door. "Hang your head in shame," is what Gene Autry and me sung to the old guy as I hauled ass out of there and into the dark.

10 🐾 Istvan Fallok

8 January 2004. I stood there and watched her go out of the door; I couldn't think of anything useful to do. All kinds of feelings were churning around inside me. Blood was a practical necessity for Justine. Mine had worked for her and I guessed that her reconstituted system would accept any type. What she was doing now was certainly the simplest and most direct way of getting what she needed; thinking about it, imagining her sinking her teeth into the neck of her first victim, excited me and filled me with a kind of perverse pride. I hoped she'd leave whomever she drank from enough blood to be going on with but I couldn't help worrying a little about her ability to restrain herself.

While I waited for Justine to return I played back our brief history. Today was the 8th of January, so it was just over a week ago, on New Year's Day, that I did a tiny Justine in a test tube. And it was on the 2nd of January that I began my preparations for the full-size primordial soup for the full-size woman. I googled for Port of London, and trawling eastward down the Thames on the website map I found TDG European Chemicals in Halfway Reach by Old Man's Head. Names to conjure with. They put me on to Gainsford Drums in Walthamstow and Bob was my uncle. When the drum was delivered I stood looking at it for a while, thinking about what would come out of the soup.

The 6th of January was the big day. When I got to the point of zapping the soup I hesitated. What if nothing happened? This, after all, was the first moment of the rest of my life. What would my life be if this moment was a failure? The idea of Justine had got into my old man's head and by now she was my without-which-nothing. "Please," I said as the 240-volt juice hit the soup, "be there!"

And she *was* there. I'd imagined her rising naked from the soup like Aphrodite but she was fully clothed in her El Paso costume. The sight of a full-size live monochrome woman was something of a shock to me and she was in a similar state. "Wha?" she said. "Where? Who?" She was very weak, and I had to hold her up to keep her from collapsing.

"First, let's get you out of these wet clothes," I said.

"Who," she said, "you?"

"That's right," I said. "Nobody here but you and me."

"Who you?"

"Istvan. You can call me Ish."

"Talk funny, you."

"I'm English. This is London."

"London, Texas?"

"England."

She shook her head. "The gold," she said, "don't let them."

"Don't worry about it, I'm taking care of everything."

"El Paso. Tornillo. Hit stage."

"Nobody's going to hit the stage," I said.

"You," she said as her shirt came off, "stop."

"It's OK, you have nothing to worry about." Actually, her monochrome brassière and then her naked breasts were not at all erotic. Quite the opposite. Dead white skin, gray nipples.

"You," she said, "not in this movie. Go way."

"This is the only movie there is," I said, "and I'm the leading man."

"Shit," she said, and fell asleep or fainted. The reality of this whole thing was nothing like what I'd anticipated. I was trying to remember why I'd been so smitten with her, so much in love that I'd had to bring her out of death and video into my primordial soup. I saw a whole lot of problems looming ahead of me while she lay there sleeping the sleep of the undead.

I hadn't really thought through the problems of having a monochromatic companion. It wasn't just the lack of color – in black-and-white she had no strength, could barely drag one foot after the other. Yesterday when I took her out all bundled up proved to me that color was the only answer, so I rang up my nephew Arkan Vulvic who's a nurse at St Eustace and asked him to get me a blood transfusion kit. Everything but the blood, which I thought would be pushing it. I've got him enough special deals on electronic equipment to make it hard for him to say no but he sounded a little worried. "Nothing illegal, I hope," he said.

"Of course not," I said. "You know me – always fooling around with one thing and another." Without asking more questions he sent me plastic bags, tubing, needles, cannulas and instructions by messenger. That was when I transferred about a pint of vintage Fallok to Justine. I felt a little strange afterwards but she was looking great and she didn't say no when I wanted what lovers want. It was disappointing.

Now she was out on her first hunt. I sat there waiting for her and picturing it in various ways. Would she suddenly sprout fangs and would her eyes light up as in the movies? No, it would be more erotic, more subtle, lingering kisses and soft caresses until she would bend to his (or indeed her) neck, brush it with her lips, then sigh and drink her fill. I almost envied the victim.

I waited and drank Irv's whiskey with a minimum of water. The hours passed; I dozed in my chair and didn't wake up until after three when she waltzed in, plumped herself down in my lap, and gave me a big wet kiss with a lot of tongue. "Wake up, Uncle Istvan," she said, "I'm hot to trot." Her cheeks were rosy, her eyes were sparkling and she was wearing a Guernsey instead of the jacket she'd left in.

"Tell me what happened," I said.

"Later – first I want a little action. Give it to me good and

I'll come in Technicolor for you." She was out of her clothes and on top of me in a flash and I have to say it was a whole lot better than the first time. She sounded as if she was enjoying it too. "Well, shut my mouth, I'm a-headin' south on the Dixie Cannonball," she sang, "Hoo-ee!" After she settled down she kissed me and said, "How was it for you, old buddy?"

"It was great. How come you're being so nice to me?"

"I told you, I'm hot to trot and right now you're what I've got. You can get back in the saddle any time you want."

"Thank you, I'll just rest for a bit. Tell me about your evening. But first I want to know where you left my jacket and where you got that jumper."

"Jumper?"

"That sweater you're wearing."

"I'll get to that," she said, "but first I have to tell you what came before." Snuggling up to me in my chair, she took my hand and placed it on her breast. "Feel the excitement in me," she murmured. "What a night!"

"Tell."

"When I went up those steps out to the street I was weak as a kitten and the whole world seemed to be losing color along with me. I was leaning against a wall feeling as if I'd been dipped in shit three times and pulled out twice when a woman came walking by. She stopped when she saw me. "Are you all right?" she said. I shook my head and she came closer. She was wearing a red jacket. She was pretty, she smelled good, she was plump and juicy. I was about to fall down but she grabbed me before I did. "I've got you," she said. "Thank you," I said. I was going to kiss her on the cheek but she turned her head so that I kissed her on the mouth. Such soft lips, and she was kissing me back with her tongue in my mouth. Her jacket was open at the top and there was the smooth bare skin of her neck and she smelled so good as I went for it. She gave a little sigh as she felt my teeth, almost as if she'd been expecting it, then she gasped as the blood began to come. I thought I would drink just enough to get me back on my feet but I couldn't stop, and as she got weaker I held her tighter. She never said anything after that one little sigh, just surrendered completely. Telling about it now I get aroused all over again – I'd never had anything in my life like the thrill of holding her close and taking what I wanted. It made me wet and squirmy, and while I was drinking there were strong colors all around me, I could hear distant voices and street sounds as if they were next to me and I could smell Chinese food and hamburgers miles away. Then suddenly there was nothing left in her. I was so sad because I hadn't meant to take her life. I carried her down some steps and left her there. I looked in her handbag to see what her name was. It was Rose, I'll always remember her, my first. I didn't take any money or anything from her and I left her bag with her."

"Next time take their ID."

"What's ID?"

"Driver's licence, that kind of thing."

"What for?"

"So the police won't know who it is right off when they find the body. You left her close to here?"

"Just a few doors down. I could have slung her over my shoulder and taken her somewhere else but I didn't want to attract attention."

"What happened to my anorak?"

"What's an anorak?"

"The jacket you had on when you left my place."

"It had some blood on it so I stuck it in a garbage can."

"We call them dustbins. Where?"

"I don't know. What does it matter?"

"My keys were in one of the pockets, on a keyring with a little torch that had 'Hermes Soundways' printed on it."

"What's Hermes Soundways?"

"This studio, this place where we are right now. And even if the keys are lost the anorak can be traced back to me, so I'd like to find that dustbin. Where did you go after you left Rose?"

"I don't know. After a while there was a big wide street with lots of lights and people and buses."

"Oxford Street?"

"Don't know."

"Did you dump the anorak before you got to the big wide street or after?"

"Not sure."

"Where did you acquire the Guernsey, before the big wide street or after?"

"What Guernsey? Cattle?"

"The jumper you're wearing, the sweater."

"Man gave it to me, I was cold."

"And what did you give him?"

"What he wanted."

"Before big wide or after?"

"After, I think."

I was beginning to see a life of endless worry unwinding ahead of me. I could see the classic scene where the police pathologist says, "There's absolutely no blood in this body, and look at those bite marks on the neck." I could see them coming down my steps and knocking on my door. I shook myself and pulled myself together. "We have to move the body," I said. "Put some clothes on and let's go."

When we got to where Rose was I looked down at her pretty face all pale and dead and I felt sad. I'd turned Justine loose on London and this was the result. The name on her Visa card was Rose Harland. "Rose Harland on her Sundays out / Walked with the better man..." I said as the Housman poem came to mind.

"Did you know her?" said Justine.

"No. Let's get her out of here."

Justine picked her up as if she weighed nothing and carried her up the steps. We propped her up against a wall and while Justine held her there I went to Berwick Street for a taxi. We pretended Rose was drunk and took her to a street near Euston Station where we left her at the bottom of some other steps. There were a few drops of blood on the collar of her jacket so I removed the jacket and put it in my rucksack. I left the empty handbag with her.

Next we searched the streets north of Oxford Street and got dirty and smelly but didn't find the anorak. "Before" and "after" describe time and space but do not necessarily mean south and north. After an hour or so I realized that our efforts were useless so we went back to my place. Justine was still full of her adventures. "I tell you, it was some kind of a rush," she said. "The world was roaring in my ears and I thought if I didn't get laid soon I'd drag some passerby into an alley and rape him. I was shivering with the cold and wondering what to do next when this guy came up to me and said, 'You look cold.' 'What about it,' I said. 'I could warm you up,' he said. 'Less talk, more action,' I said. We went to his place which was nearby and that's where I got the Guernsey."

"Did you. . .?"

"I didn't harm him. I wore him out with sex but that was all I did. He was OK when I left and sleeping like a baby. I had one more go-around with another man I met – I didn't hurt him either – and then I came home. Now I'm really hungry."

I made scrambled eggs for her and she wolfed them down, then she ran to the loo and vomited. "Maybe I drank too fast before," she said. I gave her some toast and she kept that down. "I think what I need now is sleep," she said. She undressed and climbed into bed and I tucked her in and kissed her goodnight.

Lying there she looked so sweet and pretty that for a

moment I felt as I did when I fell in love with her. Everything was different now – our reality was so hedged about with practical detail that I always had the uneasy feeling of having forgotten something important. Nothing would be simple from now on, and I was wondering if I mightn't be too old for reactivating dead women from videotapes. I went down to the studio but didn't turn on the lights. I raised the blinds and there was enough light from the street for me to see by. I poured myself some Bowmore's and added about a thimbleful of water. As my insides lit up I tried to think seriously about life, the universe and everything but only pictures came into my head: Justine with Rose Harland; Justine with Man No. 1 and Man No. 2. As fast as I faded them to black they reappeared with full sound effects.

Someone was coming down the steps: Grace Kowalski. She peered through the glass and then knocked. I couldn't evade her indefinitely so I opened the door and let her in. "Hi, Istvan," she said. "How's it going?"

"Unsimply," I said.

"Can I have some of whatever you're drinking?"

"No vodka," I said, and gave her the Bowmore's, a glass, and some water from the tap. "Cask strength," I said. "Be careful."

She mixed herself a drink, sampled it, and choked for a while. "What happens now?" she said when she could speak.

"With what?" I said. "With whom?"

"With you and your OAP totty. Does she make you feel young again?"

"That's not quite how I'd put it, Grace."

"That's *where* you'd put it, though."

"Grace, where is all this anger coming from? It's not as if you and I are an old married couple."

"That's right, we're nothing really, are we." She finished her drink, choked some more, and went out, slamming the door.

11 🐀 Chauncey Lim

9 JANUARY 2004. I saw Justine Trimble commit murder last night. I'd been keeping an eye on Fallok's place when I saw her come out. In full color, which was startling. After reaching the street she leaned against a building for a few minutes, and then a woman who was passing spoke to her. Suddenly, before you could say "Chow Yun Fat", Justine had the other woman in a close embrace. They stayed like that for perhaps ten minutes; then the other woman slumped to the street and Justine picked her up, slung her over her shoulder, carried her about half-way down the block, went down some area steps with her, came back up without her and walked away.

I hurried to where she'd left her victim. The woman was young and pretty, white as a sheet and stone-cold dead. Very sad but there was nothing I could do for her so I hurried after Justine. I followed her up Marshall to Great Marlborough Street where she took off her anorak and stuffed it into a dustbin. I retrieved it because you never know. I followed Justine as far as Oxford Street but there I lost her in the crowd. I took no further action because Rightnow is a good dog but Notyet is a safer bet.

10 January 2004. Next day I still hadn't worked out my next move so I went up to Golders Green hoping for inspiration from Rosalie Chun at Elijah's Lucky Dragon. "My goodness, Chaunce," she said, "you look as if you've seen the Malach ha-Mavet."

"Who's that when he's at home?" I said.

"The Angel of Death."

"That's pretty close to the mark. I think I need something strong, Rosalie."

"You got it, bro. I'm giving you cheese blintzes Jackie Chan with special kick-ass cottage cheese. If I tell you the secret ingredient I'll have to kill you, so don't ask."

"Who's asking?" I said. "Just lay them on me."

Rosalie does not make exaggerated claims for her food. The blintzes put new heart into me but I still wasn't sure what my next move should be. I'd seen what I'd seen, and Justine had definitely offed someone. Should I turn her in? I'm ashamed to say that if Justine had been ugly I'd probably have acted as a good citizen should. But she wasn't ugly, she was adorable-looking, and I didn't want to think of her behind bars. "Rosalie," I said. "I don't know what to do."

"What's the problem?" she said.

"It's a moral question," I said, "involving someone I know."

"This is something big, yes?"

"Yes."

"Talk to Elijah," said Rosalie. "Moral, financial, whatever, Elijah's your man."

"You mean the prophet Elijah?"

"That's the one."

"He took off for heaven in a chariot of fire," I said. "Surely he's retired now?"

"No, he's not," said Rosalie. "You know why this restaurant is called Elijah's Lucky Dragon?"

"Not yet."

"It was The Lucky Dragon before I owned it but it wasn't lucky. Back in 1982 the owner wanted to sell it for 150,000 pounds. I had 4,000 in savings but I couldn't get a mortgage for the rest. This was before I was married. Elijah appeared to me in a dream, he looked like a tramp. 'Is that you?' I said. 'You were looking for someone else?' he said. 'No,' I said, 'you're the one I want.' 'Good,' he said, 'call it Elijah's and it'll be lucky.'

'Call what?' I said. 'The restaurant you're buying,' he said. 'Who's buying?' I said. 'I haven't got the money.' 'You'll have,' he said, 'you'll buy, and you'll put my name on the sign so it'll be Elijah's Lucky Dragon, OK?' 'OK,' I said. 'Now what?' 'Who knows?' he said, 'But you can bet your arse on Elijah, I was always a fast runner.' I woke up and looked in the paper and it was the Grand National that day. There was no horse called Elijah but I found First Kings at a hundred to one so I got my 4,000 out of the bank and went to Ladbrokes and put it on First Kings to win.

"There was a man standing behind me at the window, shorter than me and Chinese. I could tell that he liked my looks. 'Who'd you bet on?' he said. 'First Kings,' I said. 'First Kings is a hundred to one,' he said, 'you're a plunger.' 'The name excites me,' I said. He nodded as if he understood that. 'Same odds as Foinavon when he won it in sixty-seven,' he said. 'How much did you bet?' 'Four thousand,' I said. 'I think you're lucky,' he said, 'so I'll do the same, and if we win let's go somewhere for drinks and dinner.' First Kings finished first and we won 800,000 pounds between us, Lester Chun and I. We had dinner at Mr Chow and Lester said, "'What shall we do with all this money?'"

Rosalie looked around at the dining room. "This is what we did with some of it," she said. "Elijah done good for us."

"Right," I said, "but does he take on non-Jewish clients?"

"Elijah is a stranger himself," said Rosalie, "so he's always ready to help a stranger. What've you got to lose?"

"OK," I said, "I'll try for an Elijah dream." I wasn't expecting anything to happen very soon but on the way home I fell asleep on the train and dreamt that it was raining and I was standing under a bridge. Another man came in out of the rain, he looked like a homeless person. "I wasn't expecting rain this week," he said.

"Are you Elijah?" I said.

"Who wants to know?" he said.

"I'm Chauncey Lim," I said. "Rosalie Chun's a friend of mine."

"You don't look Jewish," he said.

"I'm not," I said, "but I'm a stranger and I've got a question."

"OK," he said. "What's your question?"

When I told him, he said, "Nobody likes a snitch, Chaunce."

"So I shouldn't tell the police?"

"I'll have to think about this, OK? Leave it with me."

Well, I thought as I woke up, that's one less decision to make.

12 🐸 Detective Inspector Hunter

9 JANUARY 2004. When I arrive at the scene of a homicide
the usual Scene of Crime crowd are standing around waiting
for me to say something and it gets harder and harder to say
anything original. Almost everything has been said before,
a lot of it in films. By now I could mime the words while a
soundtrack says them. Right, so I got called to this Euston
crime scene at 02:25 because the medical examiner, Harrison
Burke, was all excited about the case. When I got there it was
all flashing lights and yellow tape and I stood looking down
at the body and thinking how sad it was that her young life
had been taken from her. "Any witnesses?" I said, knowing
there wouldn't be. There weren't. Then Burke said one of
those Hammer Horror film lines: "There is absolutely no
blood in this body, and look at those bite marks on the neck."

"Burke," I said in my best DI voice, "are you saying what I
think you're saying?"

"What do you think I'm saying?" he said.

"That all the blood in this body has been sucked out through
the holes in the neck?"

"That's pretty much it, John. You got it in one."

"I don't want this part of it to be leaked to the press," I said.

"There's nothing left to leak," he said, having his little joke.
"They've already done the photos, and if you're all through
here I'll get back to the lab and make my report tomorrow."

"Any ID?" I said to the sergeant who'd been first on the
scene.

"Only this," he said, and gave me an electricity bill, "and keys
in her pocket. No wallet, no handbag." The bill was to Rose
Harland at an address in Beak Street. A couple of detectives

had already been round there and they reported that she lived alone and had moved in about two months ago. The neighbors didn't know anything about her except that she was very quiet, always had a smile, and seemed to have no fixed hours for her comings and goings.

The sadness of Rose Harland's death was depressing me. "I hope this is a one-off and not the beginning of something really ugly," I said, half to myself.

Burke stopped packing up his gear and gave me a long look. "Come on, John," he said, "you've seen enough movies to know better than that. We're talking garlic-on-windows time here."

"Maybe you are," I said, "but I'm not getting ready to sharpen any stakes yet. There are all kinds of cultists and wannabes running around and they get up to all kinds of things."

"Indeed they do, and I'm betting that we'll have another case like this before too long."

"You always expect the worst, Harry."

"And that's what I generally get. I'm off. See you around."

I looked at Rose Harland's face again just before they covered it and took her away. Her lips were slightly parted, as if for a kiss. Where did I remember that name from? "Rose Harland on her Sundays out ... te-tum te-tum te-tum. Walked with the better man." Housman. She'll never walk with anyone again, poor thing. What sort of a person could do this to her?

I went on TV with an appeal for anyone who had seen her last night to come forward and tell us what they could. There were the usual useless calls but there was one from a woman who'd seen a young woman take off her anorak and drop it in a dustbin in Great Marlborough Street. "I thought it odd," she said, "because it was a cold night and she was left with only a shirt." You never know when a connection will pluck at your sleeve so I sent Sergeant Locke to Great Marlborough Street with two men. The dustbins hadn't yet been emptied and they looked into all of them but found no anorak. There was a set of keys, however, on a keyring with a little torch bearing the name of Hermes Soundways in Dufour's Place. I thought I might look in there later.

While I was waiting for Locke's report I went to Rose Harland's flat in Beak Street above the red neon sign of the Soho Pizzeria. The sparsity of her possessions was unusual: very few clothes in the cupboard, one pair of shoes with medium heels, one pair of Adidas trainers; no letters, no diary; a Letts monthly tablet calendar on the wall with the days crossed off up to the day of her death, nothing written in the daily spaces; a copy of *The Bridge of San Luis Rey* by Thornton Wilder and *The Collected Poems of A. E. Housman.* In the Housman there was a Post-it on page fifty-two and the last stanza of *A Shropshire Lad* XLVIII was bracketed:

Ay, look: high heaven and earth ail from the prime
> foundation;
All thoughts to rive the heart are here, and all in vain:
Horror and scorn and hate and fear and indignation –
> Oh why did I awake? When shall I sleep again?

In *The Bridge of San Luis Rey* page 130 was flagged and these words were underlined: "... he called twice upon St Francis, and leaning upon a flame he smiled and died."

I stood there for a while with the two books in my hand. There was a slight fragrance in the room, not so much of perfume, I thought, as of Rose Harland herself.

13 🐗 Istvan Fallok

9 JANUARY 2004. When I finally climbed into bed beside Justine after that eventful night I was tired but not sleepy. I lay there for a long time looking at her lying on her back and snoring. She was wearing my pajamas and looked touchingly vulnerable. Her color was wonderful although her breath stank. I don't think she moved all night although I tossed and turned a lot. There wasn't that much of the night left to get through and eventually a new day arrived although it felt more used than new.

I went out for bagels and I made coffee when I got back. When I went upstairs Justine was sitting up in bed and rocking back and forth with her head in her hands. She looked up all wild-eyed when I came in. "Oh, please," she moaned, "let it all be a horrible dream! But it wasn't a dream and I can taste the blood in my mouth. Why couldn't you let me stay dead! What have you done? I'm a Frankenstein monster in cowboy boots."

"We have to get you some clothes," I said. "You can't wear the same ones day after day and you're kind of conspicuous in that outfit unless a rodeo comes to town."

"How could I do what I did!" she went on. "She clung to me while I sucked the life out of her. Ugh! I'm a monster now and all I have to look forward to is more of the same, hunting night after night and coming home with blood in my mouth. Maybe I won't do any more hunting and I'll just die quietly. This is no kind of a life." She began to sob.

"You were feeling pretty good about it last night," I said.

She shook herself as if she could get it off her back. "That was some kind of vampire binge," she said. "It was all that

blood that I drank so fast, it was the blood talking, not me."
She managed to eat a toasted bagel and drink some black coffee without throwing up, and then she calmed down and settled into a quiet depression.

I didn't know how long she could go without a fresh sup-
ply of blood and I was dreading the next time she'd need
some. Maybe I'd have to go with her to make sure she didn't
completely drain the victim. In the meantime I wasn't
returning phone calls and nothing was happening at Hermes
Soundways except vampire work. Oh, to be back in my regular life where I'd get up in the morning looking forward to
the day's technical problems!

14 🐿 Chauncey Lim

10 JANUARY 2004. When I turned up at Fallok's place he said, "What?"

"What indeed," I said. "That's a very warm greeting for the guy who showed you how to reconstitute Justine Trimble."

"I've got a lot on my mind," he said.

"I don't doubt it. What the hell kind of recipe did you use for Justine? I was there when she committed murder."

He looked as if he might pick up something heavy and beat me to death with it. "What are you going to do about it?" he said.

"I don't know. I just dropped in to see what condition my condition was in."

"And what condition *is* it in?"

"I'm not sure. I've got this bloodstained anorak she left in a dustbin in Great Marlborough Street. The police are probably looking for it. Here, take it."

He took it, felt in all the pockets, shook his head and said, "Shit. No keys."

"The anorak is just as I found it," I said. "I didn't take anything out of the pockets."

"Never mind. What do you want, Chauncey?"

"First of all, I want to know what's happening. After that it's negotiable."

"You said you saw her commit murder. Did you see how she did it?"

"No, I wasn't close enough. I saw the other woman slump down but I didn't know she was dead until I had a closer look."

"She was dead," said Istvan, "because Justine sucked all the blood out of her."

"Oh my God! You mean...?"

"That's what I mean, Chaunce."

"Oh dear, oh dear, oh dear. From the seed of trouble grows the trouble tree. What now?"

"You tell me. Are you in or out?"

"In or out of what?"

"Still fancy Justine?"

"Crikey, I don't know. This puts her in a whole new light. Or darkness, rather."

"Doesn't it just! Do you want a piece of the action or not?"

"You'll have to be more explicit – I'm not up to speed on this."

"It's like this, Chaunce: she's already got a pint of my blood in her plus what she got on her own but she'll need topping up from time to time and I'm going to have to subcontract some of the work. If you want to join the Justine club you'll have to give her some of what it takes. Like the fellow said, 'the blood is the life'."

"And in return?"

"You get what you've been craving for. Justine is a treat to look at when she's been hematologically refreshed and she'll be very affectionate, I promise you."

"My God, you're pimping for her."

"Needs must when the Devil drives, Chaunce. You can take the high moral ground or you can follow your heart."

"My *heart*, for Christ's sake!"

"Or whatever part is leading you. We're talking pragmatism here."

"We certainly are, and I'm a little breathless from it."

"Perfectly understandable. Take your time, think about it: five, ten minutes, whatever. She's young, she's beautiful in full color, she's longing for what you've got."

"Is she here now? Could I see her?"

"Absolutely. She's just having a kip. She needs lots of rest."

45

He led the way to the bedroom and there she was, nude, only partly covered by the duvet. I looked at her shoulder, her beautiful bottom and the leg she stretched out. She rolled over, exposing her breasts, and opened her eyes. "Who's this?" she said.

"This is Chauncey," said Istvan. "He's going to be your new uncle if you treat him right."

"Hi, Chauncey," she said. "You look some livelier than Ish. Are you ready for a little uncle work?"

"I thought you'd never ask," I said.

15 🐹 Irving Goodman

10 JANUARY 2004. Why do I so often have that left-out feeling? Because I'm so often left out, that's why. The grown-up is only a thin coat of chocolate over the hard nut of the child. Whatever you were as a kid, you still are when the chocolate gets licked off or scraped off. When they used to choose up sides for baseball or any other game I was always left till the last.

I went to Fallok's place and looked in through the glass and there was Justine in glorious Technicolor sitting on some Chinese guy's lap while Fallok was tinkering with an oscilloscope. So he was back at work in his normal routine and there were the three of them all cosy. I could scarcely believe it. "Yo, Istvan!" I said. Childhood again. When I was a kid and we wanted somebody to come out and play, we stood outside the house and yelled, "Yo, Bob!" or whatever his name was.

Fallok stuck his head out of the second-story window of childhood and said, "Hi, Irv. Hey, I've been meaning to call you but I got so far behind in my work that it's been all I could do to catch up. What do you think of our girl? Isn't she looking great?"

"*Our* girl," I said. "*Our* girl is exactly what she isn't. You were meant to bring her into flesh-and-blood 3-D for *me*, not for you and your friend."

"My name is Chauncey Lim," the friend said. "Try not to lose tranquillity. 'A bow long bent waxes weak.' One is divisible by three and it adds up to a good deal all round."

"Do me a favor," I said: "stuff it up your fortune cookie."

"How's that arrangement sound to you, Justine?" said Fallok.

"Are you kidding?" she said. "I doubt if this old drynuts even has half a pint in him."

I couldn't imagine why I'd ever thought I was in love with this woman. On the screen she'd had a wholesome kind of outdoor refinement but now the hang of her face was definitely sluttish.

"First of all," said Fallok to me, "I clearly remember telling you that I couldn't promise anything. I said that because I knew from experience that life is full of surprises. Secondly, we had no kind of contract, oral or written; I simply said I'd see what I could do."

"We've seen that all right," I said. "After that sighting of you and your bundled-up tootsie that night I thought we'd have some kind of a meeting but you haven't been answering your phone and every time I've come here the door's been locked and the blinds have been down. I couldn't get any news from Grace and here I am again and here you lot are and you're all right, Jack. Bloody hell."

"Look," said Fallok, "let's try to be grown-up about this, OK? What we have here isn't quite the usual boy-girl thing and it calls for a more sophisticated approach."

"I'm not even sure I want to approach it any more," I said. "I'm beginning to feel myself backing away from it."

"I'm heartbroken," said Justine. "but maybe there's new blood coming our way unless it's the Avon lady."

Everybody looked at the door and listened but we saw and heard nothing. "Justine's senses are sharper than ours," said Fallok. After about a minute there were two men coming down the steps.

"It's the Bill," said Chauncey.

There was a knock at the door and Fallok answered it. "I'm Detective Inspector Hunter," said a tall man with a deep voice and a Victorian moustache. He showed us his warrant card. "This is Sergeant Locke." Locke's tumblers clicked and he nodded. Hunter looked at us as if he knew all our little secrets and right away I felt guilty.

"Istvan Fallok," said Fallok. "What can I do for you?"

"Are you the proprietor of Hermes Soundways?" said Hunter.

"I am," said Istvan.

Hunter swept all of us with his eyes like a beam from a lighthouse. "Do any of you know a woman called Rose Harland?" he said

We all shook our heads and said no. "What about Rose Harland?" said Fallok.

"Later," said Hunter. "Are these your keys?" He gave them to Fallok.

"Yes," said Fallok. "Where'd you find them?"

"Where'd you lose them?" said Hunter.

"Somewhere between here and Oxford Street, I think. On the way to HMV."

Hunter nodded. "We found them in a dustbin in Great Marlborough Street. Any idea how they got there?"

"No," said Fallok.

"Where were you on the evening of Thursday the eighth of January?" said Hunter. "Day before yesterday."

"Here," said Fallok.

"What do you do here at Hermes Soundways?" said Hunter.

"Sounds in different ways," said Fallok. "Would you like to hear some?"

"Yes, I would," said Hunter.

"This is from *Laminations on a Theme of Cthulhu* by Fathoms," said Fallok, and started the music. "It's a low-frequency enhancement," he said as the sound, mostly subsonic vibrations, made our bones rattle.

"Deep," said Hunter. "Very hermetic."

"Most of what I do is," said Fallok modestly.

"Yes," said Hunter. "May I ask who your friends are?"

"Chauncey Lim," said Chauncey.

"And where were you on the Tuesday in question?" said Hunter.

"Working late at my shop in D'Arblay Street," said Chauncey. "I do photographic novelties."

Hunter looked at him as if he'd heard that sort of euphemism before, but passed on to me.

"Irving Goodman," I said. "I was at home in Fulham, Kempson Road. I'm retired."

"From what?" said Hunter.

"TV writing."

Hunter turned to Justine.

"Justine Trimble," she said. "I was here with Istvan."

"Doing what?"

"Nothing much, just what people do."

"Where are you from, Ms Trimble?" said Hunter.

"Texas."

"And your occupation?"

"I'm an actress. I'm. . ."

"The daughter of Justine Trimble who starred in so many westerns back in the 1950s," said Fallok.

"Unusual for the daughter to have the same name as the mother," said Hunter.

"Yes, I'm Justine Trimble Jr," said Justine. "I'm not a big star. Mostly I appear at motor shows and conventions."

"Can I see your passport, please?" said Hunter.

"It was stolen when she got mugged the other night," said Fallok.

"Where did this happen?" said Hunter to Justine.

"Argyll Street," said Fallok.

"Please let the lady speak for herself," said Hunter. "When did it happen, Ms Trimble?"

"Between eight and nine," said Justine. "Night before last."

"That would be Thursday the eighth of January?"

"Yes."

"Give the details of the incident to Sergeant Locke and we'll get it into the system. You should go to the United States Embassy and they can issue you with a new passport if you can show proof of your identity."

"Yes," said Justine.

"I assume you have such proof?"

"Everything was stolen when I got mugged," said Justine.

"Where was your birth registered?"

"El Paso."

"When?"

"Twenty-five years ago."

"Nineteen seventy-nine," said Hunter.

"Yes."

"Where is your birth certificate now?"

"At home."

"Which is where?"

"Tornillo."

"Is there someone there who can be contacted?"

"No, I live alone."

"Right. Well, if you go to the embassy I'm pretty sure they can get this sorted. How long are you here for?"

"Three weeks," said Fallok. "She's staying with me."

"Yes," said Hunter. He looked at all of us as if he would have preferred to lock us up but he contented himself with paying close attention while Justine gave the rest of her mugging details to Sergeant Locke which took about thirty seconds. Then Hunter nodded and they started to go but when he was half-way out the door he did a Columbo. With his back to us he stopped and raised his left arm as if he'd been brought to a halt. "Oh," he said, "there's just one more thing."

"What?" said Fallok.

Hunter turned to face us and looked apologetic. "If you don't mind, I'd like to take saliva samples from the four of you."

"What for?" said Fallok.

"I don't know," said Hunter. "It's a new procedure the medical examiner keeps nagging us about. It'll only take a few minutes of your time." From his pocket he produced four plastic tubes, each containing a swab. We opened our mouths in turn, he did his swabbing, replaced the swabs and stoppered and labeled the tubes one by one, said, "There we are," and left.

"What was all that about?" I said.

"Obviously they want to match up some DNA sample they've got," said Fallok, looking at Justine, "and you can be sure they'll be back again. In any case, we're fucked. It'll take Hunter about ten minutes to establish that Justine is technically and officially a non-person and that's when the shit hits the fan."

"I'll be damned if I'll go to jail," said Justine. "I didn't ask to be here. I didn't even ask to *be*. I think I was better off dead."

I was wondering if she mightn't be right about that. "What did she mean before about half a pint?" I asked Fallok. "Half a pint of what?"

"Hello?" said Fallok. "The blood is the life?"

"What," I said, "she's a vampire?"

"No racist remarks, please," said Fallok.

"I don't want any blood from him," said Justine. "Besides which he's got none to spare."

"You wouldn't be here if it weren't for me," I said.

"That makes you Number One on my shit list," she said.

"Let's not squabble among ourselves," said Lim. "Right now we need to find a safe house for Justine."

"Any ideas?" said Fallok.

"Rosalie Chun's got a big house," said Lim, "and there's nothing to connect her to Justine."

"Sounds good," said Fallok. "Better get her out of here before Hunter pops in again."

"That OK with you, Justine?" said Lim.

"That's the first time anybody's asked my opinion about anything," she said. "Let's haul ass, Chaunce."

16 🐷 Justine Trimble

10 JANUARY 2004. Being alive after being dead for forty-seven years is weird to begin with, and it gets weirder from one minute to the next. I didn't know when I was born or when I died but Chauncey looked me up on the Internet Movie Database and found that I was born in 1932 in Amarillo and I died in 1957 on location in Arizona when I was thrown by a horse. I don't remember that. I was married to an oilman named William Connors and I don't remember that either. He's probably dead by now or as good as.

When we left Hermes Soundways Chauncey took me to a place called Topshop in Oxford Circus. This was on a Saturday afternoon and Oxford Circus was full of traffic and big red buses and people and noise. Topshop was noisier inside than it was outside. The music was so loud you couldn't think and the store was full of wild-looking girls. Chauncey bought me jeans and sweatshirts, underwear and pajamas and sheepskin boots and a lilac duffel coat with lime-green lining and toggles. And a pair of leopard-print sunglasses because the sunlight hurt my eyes. "A little bit of retail therapy is always good for what ails you," he said. "How're you feeling?"

"I'm feeling pretty good," I said. "I don't think I'll need topping up today."

"Good," said Chauncey, "but we've got the transfusion kit just in case."

We took the Underground to Golders Green and it was a very long ride. There were more different kinds of people than I could remember ever seeing before: black, brown, yellow, white, and all different shades of those colors. Some of them looked at me and I wondered if they could smell what I was.

When we came out of the Underground we walked to Elijah's Lucky Dragon. It was closed for the Jewish Sabbath but Rosalie Chun was still there and she came to the door when Chauncey knocked. A big woman in one of those Chinese dresses that's slit up to the thigh. A nice face and she must have been pretty when she weighed fifty pounds less if she ever did. "What's up, Chaunce?" she said.

"I've got an emergency here, Rosalie," said Chauncey. "Can you help us?"

"Yes," said Rosalie. "What's your name, emergency?"

"Justine," I said.

"Come on in and set right down and make yourself at home," said Rosalie, and I did feel at home right away.

Chauncey explained the situation to her and he said to Rosalie, "Do you think there's any chance of weaning her on to regular food?"

"You came to the right place," said Rosalie. "Give me about half an hour in the kitchen and let's see what I can do. Don't you worry, love," she said to me. "I'll see you right."

After a while she put a bowl of broth and a plate of dumplings in front of me. "This is Golem broth," she said. "The spoon can stand up in it which is about right. And these on the plate are gosky patties Ba'al Shem Tov."

"Gosky patties are from Edward Lear," said Chauncey.

"His recipe is nonsense," said Rosalie. "Mine has been in my family for generations and it's the real thing."

"What about your North Chinese cuisine?" said Chauncey.

"There's a time for multicultural," said Rosalie, "and there's a time for going with 4,000 years of your own people." To me she said, "Eat, and be strong."

I ate and I did feel better. My momma didn't raise no vampires. I don't know how long this second life will last but however long it does I won't forget Rose Harland. I hope I don't do any more killing.

Rosalie and her husband have an apartment over the restaurant and there's a whole other apartment above that one. She and Lester Chun keep it for business visitors but it's empty now and that's where I am, thanks to Chauncey. The bed is big and soft, the sheets smell like fresh air and sunlight, there's a big comforter that they call a doovay, and the whole place is warm and cosy. From my window I can see the Kim Chee restaurant and Supersave across from us and people in the windows above them. They can all remember where they were two weeks ago. Two weeks ago there wasn't any me, I was dead and long gone.

I know I'm not real the way real people are, I'm not alive in the same way. But I *am* alive in some kind of way. I think about Rose Harland a lot. I wish I hadn't taken her life. Now I feel like she's part of me. Maybe I have to stay alive for both of us.

I've been slipping around like a regular little whore. First I let Istvan crawl on top of me and then there were those two men whose names I don't even know, then Istvan again, then Chauncey but that wasn't the same thing because he was very polite and I kind of liked him. But those others, Jesus. There's not going to be any more of that, things are going to be different from now on. Well, like the feller says, "I ain't got to where I'm going but I'm past where I been."

I get mixed up between what's a real memory and what's not. I told the inspector that I was born in Tornillo but then Chauncey told me it was Amarillo. Sometimes I thought it was Tishomingo, Oklahoma. We come out of there in a old Ford truck with everything piled up on it and tied down – mattresses and pots and pans, picks and shovels and Grandma's rocking chair. Or was that in some movie that I seen. Saw. My land, listen at how I'm talking. Sweet Jesus, help me get straight. Just a closer walk with thee, Lord, let it be.

Sometimes Rosalie and Lester have business meetings in

their apartment and then they put a parrot in this one. Flat, I have to stop saying apartment. In this flat. The parrot's name is Elijah. He's a very smart bird. When he saw me he said, "Phwoarr. Chauncey won the totty lottery." I thought totty was some kind of drink but Chauncey said that totty is a woman you go to bed with. Live and learn.

17 🐗 Detective Inspector Hunter

12 JANUARY 2004. Interesting report from Harrison Burke: "Cause of Rose Harland's death we know: all of her blood was sucked out of her body, probably by whoever made the wound in her neck. There were traces of blood and saliva on her throat and the collar of her jacket. The blood was her own; the saliva was not. DNA testing of the saliva cells on throat and jacket on 9 January showed a match with the sample taken from Istvan Fallok 10 January at Hermes Soundways. The 10 January sample taken from Justine Trimble matches that of Chauncey Lim on the same date. The sample from Irving Goodman on 10 January does not match anyone else's.

"I put Rose Harland's age at between twenty-five and thirty. Her womb shows scars of an abortion carried out approximately two months before time of death."

18 🦫 Irving Goodman

11 JANUARY 2004. There isn't just one reality, there are lots of them. No, there's just the one and it contains all the others. It's a polyhedron and each plane is a window to a different reality. What's happening now is not the same kind of reality as some I remember.

When I was little we lived thirty miles away from Philadelphia and we used to drive in on Sundays to visit our relatives. My uncle Barney had a drug store at 12th and Poplar in what was then called a "colored" neighborhood. There was a display window in which hung two amphora-shaped glass vessels suspended by chains. The one on the left contained a beautiful red liquid; the one on the right was filled with green. There is just such a drug store in a painting by Edward Hopper, with PRESCRIPTION DRUGS and EX-LAX across the top of the window. There must have been a lot of constipation at that time. The Ex-Lax slogan was "When Nature forgets, remember Ex-Lax". I don't think Uncle Barney's window said Ex-LAX. He had many customers who came in with cuts from razor fights and said, "Fix me up, Doc."

There was no soda fountain that I remember but I was often given chewing gum. The rooms behind and above the drug store were divided by bead curtains made of little pink and yellow glass sticks that clicked as you passed through them. They looked like candy. The lampshades also had little pink and yellow glass sticks hanging from them. In an upstairs bedroom lay my mother's father whom we called Zayda (Grandfather). The room smelled medicinal. He spoke no English but gave me dimes. Tante Celia was Uncle Barney's wife and Uncle Izzy, pronounced Easy, from my father's side lived there also. Uncle Easy wore a truss. My cousins Daniel and Leonard and Bobby were there too. Did we play Parcheesi? There are flavors that one tastes not with the mouth but with the mind. I taste the flavor of those Sundays as I write this: the street lamps in the evening; the brilliant red and green vessels in the illuminated window. Their reality was not the same as what I have now.

My thoughts about Justine change from moment to moment. I was naturally offended by her rejection of me but I no longer am. To be called up out of the dead as she was must be a terrifying experience and her being must be an uneasy construct of shifting realities that might collapse at any moment into nothingness. I can't imagine her memories.

19 🐿 Medical Examiner Harrison Burke

13 JANUARY 2004. John Hunter said to me, "Harry, what are you saying?"

"What's in my report," I told him, "that's what I'm saying."

"OK, so Istvan Fallok left saliva on Rose Harland's neck?"

"I didn't say that, I only said there was a match with his 10th January sample."

"So how'd his saliva get on her neck? Did he suck her blood? Is he the murderer we're looking for?"

"I can't answer that."

"And Justine Trimble's 10th January sample matches Chauncey Lim's of the same date? What about that? Heavy kissing?"

"I have no explanation for that."

"So what are you saying?"

"Just what I've said."

"That's it?"

"That's it from me."

20 🐀 Grace Kowalksi

13 JANUARY 2004. I don't like being mucked about. Istvan
Fallok and I aren't a couple but we sleep together once in a
while and we're intimate in all kinds of practical ways that
make people closer than sex does. And now he's got this dead-
meat video creature and Grace is out of the loop. Fine. Great.
But maybe I can make him sorry for that. I'm not sure how
but I'll think of something.

21 🐾 Irving Goodman

14 JANUARY 2004. Somebody once said, "You get too soon old and too late smart." I'm eighty-three now. Maybe I'll get smart when I'm dead. Today is Wednesday but it feels like the Sunday evenings of my boyhood. Darkness coming on and tomorrow is Monday and nothing to look forward to but school. Sunday evenings were the death of the weekend and here it is Sunday evening on Wednesday.

I was playing chess against myself and losing. What did I expect? I'm still opening with the Ruy Lopez just as I did at sixteen. While losing I was listening to Souad Massi's album *deb* (heartbroken):

> Oh! My heart, your wound deepens
> Oh! My heart, who is responsible for that?

There she was on the album cover, young and beautiful with her guitar and her sweet seductive voice full of sadness. Any man hearing her sing would want to cuddle her and make her feel better but I'm pretty sure her heart isn't broken. Mine is, and who is responsible for that? Justine? Not really. How could I think she would want me, what have I to offer? So here I was in the Sunday evening of my old age with a broken heart, all alone and being beaten at chess. I drank some cask strength with very little water and I felt terrible in a much classier way. Burning all the way down. "Parv," said the inner Irv.

"I know," I replied. Inner Irv says words that are meaningless but I usually know what he means.

When the phone rang I picked it up and said, "At the third stroke, the time will be exactly Sunday evening."

"Irv?" said Grace Kowalski.

"Hi, Grace," I said. "What's new?"

"It's Wednesday, Irv."

"Maybe it is where you are but here it's Sunday evening."

"Are you drunk?"

"Yes. Would you like to take advantage of me?"

"Of course, but we have serious things to talk about as well. Can you come over or shall I come to you?"

"I'll come to you – your place smells strange and beautiful like the things you make and like you."

"Irv!" she said. "Think serious."

"I'll be very serious," I said. "I'll see you shortly." Feeling almost middle-aged again, I went forth to Fulham Broadway, where millions have been spent to convert the old tube station into a Nowheresville shopping mall with Books Etc., Boots, a Virgin Megastore, Starbucks, Orange and other commercial enterprises set in a brilliantly illuminated desolation that is part of the greater program to turn London into Noplace. Shaking my head as I do each time, I took the lift down to the District Line platform and got an Edgware Road train to Notting Hill Gate where I took the Central Line to Oxford Circus. The trains were not crowded and none of the passengers were talking into little telephones or smiling as they tapped out text messages. Some were reading books or newspapers. All of the faces, young, old, male, female, white and brown and black, were part of the many faces of the great sad thing that moves itself from here to there and back again in all forms of transport.

At Oxford Circus I came up to the surface and the squalor of Argyll Street and people buying things they'd be better off not eating. *Chitty Chitty Bang Bang* was playing at the Palladium, starring Michael Ball. Well, I thought, it's nice that he has the work. Long ago I read somewhere that all of the visible world is *maya*, illusion, but whatever you call it, it's what you have to deal with. I carried on to Great Marlborough Street, then over to Berwick where I went well past Grace's place to buy a bottle of Stolichnaya at Nicolas, then back to All That Glisters.

"Yo, Grace," I said as I pressed the intercom button.

"Yo, Irv," she said, and came down to let me in. A hug and a kiss and I gave her the latest Justine news as we went up to the studio and its professional smells. The unfinished piece on her workbench was a three-legged toad in green and orange stones with an I Ching coin in its mouth.

"I got the idea for the I Ching coin from A2 Feng Shui on the internet. I don't know what's on theirs."

"What's the hexagram on yours?"

"Number forty-two, *I, Increase*, SUN CHEN, with nine at the beginning, so it changes to number twenty, *Kuan, Contemplation*, SUN K'UN."

"That's a very hopful toad, Grace."

"Where there's life, there's hop," she said, and we drank to that and sighed a little. "OK," I said. "Talk seriously to me."

"Form is emptiness and emptiness is form," she said. "You know what I'm saying?"

"Of course, *Ça va sans dire*," I said. "It walks without talking."

"That's what I like about you, Irv, everything doesn't have to be spelt out."

"So tell me, I'm all ears. Tell me while we're still coherent."

"I think," she said, "it's time for me to stop getting mad and start getting even."

"Every woman's right," I said.

"Justine," she said, "was put together from an image on videotape, yes?"

"Yes."

"Got any more Justine on tape?"

"Oho!"

"Righty-oh," said Grace, and we drank to that.

"But from the video to a walking-around Justine is a whole big project," I said, "and I have no idea where to start. Do you?"

"No, but I know a man who does and I've got keys to his place. All I need is a little time alone in Hermes Soundways and I'll find his notes. Now that Justine's up in Golders Green he'll probably drop in on her and that's when I'll do it."

"OK, say we get the whole thing figured out and we end up with Justine Number Two, have you any idea what to do next?"

"If we build her it will come. When we've got her standing in front of us the next thing will make itself known. Do you think you'll fall in love with this one too?"

"I've done that particular folly once already; I'm not likely to do it again. Besides, she's not as amazing as you are, Grace."

"You silver-tongued seducer," she said, and we retired to the bedroom with the Stolichnaya.

"Don't ever say you're not a player," said Grace as we freshened our drinks. She's very gracious.

"Well, I don't do the full orchestra," I said, "but if you like chamber music, I'm your man."

"I'll drink to that," said Grace.

Mutiny on the Bounty, the one with Clark Gable and Charles Laughton, was on TV that evening and we both enjoyed seeing it yet again. "Every now and then," I said, "I come across some mention of

Bligh in the papers where they say he wasn't all that bad."

"He was a hell of a navigator," said Grace. "Thirty-six hundred miles in an overloaded open boat!"

"And he had no charts and there were only about a week's rations," I said, "but he got them all to Timor safely."

"Well," said Grace, "he suspended his disbelief and all that remained was the belief that he could do it."

"Plus his practical knowledge and his seamanship," I said. "If I had to be cast adrift in that longboat I'd rather have Bligh at the tiller than Fletcher Christian."

"He was the man," said Grace. "No doubt about it."

All in all, a very pleasant evening and we fell asleep talking about DIY Justines.

22 🐻 Detective Inspector Hunter

18 January 2004. Harry Burke and I were drinking London Pride at The Anchor & Hope by the River Lea. A cold winter evening but we took our pints outside and sat down on a bench under the street lamp to enjoy the peacefulness of it. Across the river a train clattered with its windows all lit. It went over the bridge and the Sunday quiet moved in again behind it. Four murders, two suicides, three rapes and assorted burglaries this past week. Life goes on.

We didn't say much for a while, drinking in the quiet with the London Pride. "Well," I said, "we've had nothing new in the vampire line."

"Early days," said Burke.

"You're still expecting another one?"

"You're the detective, not me. What do *you* think?"

"I think I'd feel a lot better if we could catch whoever killed Rose Harland."

"Have you made any progress with your suspects?" He was looking at me the way he looks when he's waiting for me to catch up with his mental processes.

"Not yet," I said. "I'm pretty sure Istvan Fallok didn't kill her."

"How do you explain his saliva on her jacket?"

"I think you know what's in my mind about that, don't you?"

"Maybe," said Burke.

"Go on," I said, "say it."

"You're wondering if someone else left Fallok's saliva on Rose Harland's jacket?"

"That's right. How could that have happened?"

"And you're wondering why Justine Trimble's saliva on the 10th of January was a match with Chauncey Lim's?"

"OK, why was it?"

"This is as new to me as it is to you, but what if Justine has no cellular identity of her own?"

"Go on."

"What if she needs blood in order to survive, and Istvan Fallok gave her some before she killed Rose Harland? And Chauncey Lim topped her up before we took her saliva on the 10th of January? Tell me, am I talking nonsense?"

One of the locals came out of the pub and nodded to Burke. "All right, Harry?" he said.

"All right, Mick?" said Burke.

"Inspector," said Mick. I'm known there because Burke is local and we always go to The Anchor & Hope when I visit.

"Good evening to you," I said.

"Terrible, that vampire case," said Mick.

"What are you talking about?" I said.

"That woman as didn't have no blood left in her," said Mick.

"Don't believe everything you read in the tabloids," I said.

"Didn't read it," said Mick. "My wife works at the mortuary and she saw the body when they brought it in. Proper drained, it was. Have you got any leads?"

"I'm not able to say anything at this time," I said.

"Right you are, guv," said Mick. "Mum's the word." He nodded again and left.

"What can I say?" said Burke. "His wife does work in the mortuary."

"Small fucking world," I said.

"To get back to Justine, what do you think you'll do?"

"I think I'll have to talk to her and Fallok and Lim again and this time I'll ask better questions."

"I'm looking forward to the answers," said Burke. And on that note we finished our last pints and went home.

23 🐸 Grace Kowalski

29 JANUARY 2004. When Irv went home I felt kind of low. I dragged myself into the morning with black coffee and a stale bagel, then I sat looking at the three-legged toad on my workbench. It was commissioned by a man in his thirties who's an investment broker in the City. He makes a lot of money and wants to make a lot more. His eyes are like rivets that keep his brain in place but the rivets are a little loose by now. He showed me a drawing of Liu Hai and the toad in a book, *Chinese Symbolism and Art Motifs*. Liu Hai was a tenth-century Minister of State who hung out with this toad. Sometimes it would hide from him in a well and he'd tempt it out by lowering a string loaded with gold coins. "This toad attracts wealth," said Mr Rivet-Eyes, "and I'm going to put it in a corner diagonally opposite my front door for the best Feng Shui effect."

"Do you need more money than you have now?" I asked him.

"You always need more money," he said.

I said, "I think in cases of greed the toad might work against the one who asks for its help."

"Greed? What are you talking about? I'm not greedy – all I want is a fair share of the action."

"OK," I said. I went to the V & A to check it out and there they were on the fourth floor, Liu Hai about seven inches high in brown clay and the toad buff with brown spots. Liu Hai trying to catch the toad which was looking very sly and sneaking away with a coin in its mouth. I copied down everything on the card because you never know. It said:

Liu Hai with the three-legged toad.
Mark: Made by Xu Xiutang,
Autumn of Chengshen Year [Yixingy] 1980
FL32-1984

I liked that toad, it looked as if it had seen wealth-seekers
come and go over the centuries and was not much impressed
by them.

Another version of the three-legged toad story is that it
exists "only in the moon, which it swallows during the eclipse.
It has therefore come to be a symbol of the unattainable." That
version made more sense to me than the wealth one, and I
wondered if I wasn't helping my client to delude himself with
fantasies of wealth that he would never possess. The look on
the toad's face suggested that Mr Rivet-Eyes might well end
up with a wealth of unattainable.

But there was the matter of Justine to be considered. Irv
was waiting for me to get Istvan's notes and I was waiting
for Istvan to leave his place. On Friday the 23rd I kept a close
watch and I saw him go out. I waited a while to make sure it
wasn't only a local errand, then I read my bit of *The Heart
Sutra*, which I always do at the start of any serious enterprise:

> Here, O Sariputra. Form is emptiness and the very
> emptiness is form; emptiness does not differ from
> form, form does not differ from emptiness; whatever is
> form, that is emptiness, whatever is emptiness, that is
> form, the same is true of feelings, perceptions, impulses
> and consciousness.

I've never read the whole *Heart Sutra* but if form is emptiness,
then not reading it is the same as reading it, so I'm all right
with that one bit. It always seems to do me good, and as soon

as I say, "Here, O Sariputra," I'm up for whatever I need to do.

I let myself into Hermes Soundways and stood there listening for a few moments. Then I got to work. Istvan's filing system was simple: he just piled the most recent thing on top of the one before it. That was the main system which included invoices, receipts, and newspaper cuttings as well as notes. There were several lesser ones consisting of backs of envelopes, various scraps of paper with writing on them and the odd matchbook cover. I separated what seemed to be Justine material from everything else, put it into what I thought might be chronological order and bundled it into the bag I'd brought with me.

Hoping not to run into Istvan I went down Dufour's to Broadwick and over to Berwick. When The Blue Posts pub and red-and-yellow Nicolas and the Fine Crêpes wagon with its yellow scallop-edged canopy came into view I was on my home turf and I breathed easier. GOOD NEWS, said the sign above the red *Newsweek* awning at the start of my stretch of Berwick. At Nicolas I bought a bottle of Stolichnaya, then paused at the blue canvas-roofed flower stand diagonally opposite for some yellow and mauve chrysanthemums. For a moment the smell of roast chestnuts came back to me from long-gone Decembers. Careful not to step on the cracks in the pavement I made my way back to All That Glisters past my many competitors in the jewelry line and my various landmarks: Reckless Records; then Badge Sales which looks like a message drop in a thriller; above it is a tailor with a blue plaque on his window:

TOM BAKER
1966–2041
BESPOKE TAILOR
Works here but lives
around the corner

How did he calculate his life span? Will he top himself at
seventy-five or what? One day I'll ask him but I keep putting it
off. The Cotton Café, The Maharani Indian Tandoori Restaurant with its splendid yellow sign (Maharani in red), followed
after a decent interval by the Raj Tandoori Restaurant, also
with a yellow sign like a beacon of Eastern heat in the English
winter. Then I was home.

Up in the studio I poured myself a drink and sat down on
the floor with my load of whatever it was. As I held the papers
in my hand an invoice fell out. I took that as a sign that something was trying to tell me something. The invoice was from
Thierson & Bates Biologicals in Surrey for *Rana temporaria*
(3), £33. I rang up Thierson & Bates and said I was Mr Fallok's secretary. "I'm going through invoices for his VAT
return," I said, "and I'm not sure about this one from you.
What are three *Rana temporaria*?"

"Common frogs," said the man at the other end.

"Right," I said. "I assume these were. . . ?"

"Laboratory-quality specimens in formaldehyde," said the
man.

"Oh, yes," I said, "Now I remember the project. Thanks
very much."

The next thing was a handwritten recipe for primordial
soup which included 20 gallons of chicken noodle, 500 Oxo
cubes, 500mg of polypeptides, 40 bottles of Ring-Bo-Ree (an
obvious codename) plus quantities of ginseng and assorted
multivitamins.

It was the polypeptides that convinced me that I was well
out of my depth so I rang up Irv and asked him to come over.
He came with a new bottle, sensitive human being that he is,
and we looked the whole lot over togezzer. Together. "Well,"
he said, "it's a good thing that I have a nephew who's a poly-
math. He knows everything."

"I don't care if he's a merphradomite," I said. "Bring him on."

So the next day or some other day Artie Nussbaum turned up. He's at the Guy's, King's & St Thomas' School of Medicine and he's good with chemistry, biology and computers. He's a little guy and he looks as if you added water you'd have four or five Charlie Sheens.

"Oho," he said when he looked through what we had. "Is this legal?"

"Artie," said Irv, "are you going to ask dumb questions or are you going to help your uncle?"

"Sorry," he said. To me he said, "Have you got a computer with a modem?"

I led him to the computer and he sighed and said, "If you could order me a pizza with pepperoni and a six-pack of John Smith?"

"No prob," I said. I got him what he needed and we left him to it. He had to go to lectures from time to time but after three days he gave us a shopping list for all kinds of things plus three *Rana temporaria*. We ordered the laser gear, the extra computer software, the oil drum and the rest of it. For the primordial soup there was the matter of the forty bottles of Ring-Bo-Ree. Artie was not bothered about that. "What we're doing here," he said, "is creating a suspension of disbelief in which the visual particles of Justine Two will be held pending the zapping which will precipitate the whole woman. For Ring-Bo-Ree read any high-calorie filler that will enhance the body of the soup, say John Smith, forty cans of."

"Julv," said Irv.

"Sorry?" said Artie.

"Just thinking out loud," said Irv. "I agree that John Smith can go in for Ring-Bo-Ree."

I did too, so that was one less problem. When we got to *Rana temporaria* Thierson & Bates said, "Sorry, we're temporarily out of frogs. Would you like some other batrachian?"

"Like what?" I said.

"Toads?" said the man. "I can do you some nice *Bufo bufo* in formaldehyde."

"Yes," I said, going all goosepimply, "those will do nicely."

24 🐹 Artie Nussbaum

30 JANUARY 2004. OK, so I didn't ask dumb questions. Actually, after a while I became completely involved in what I was doing and I stopped worrying about legality and morality. Like the guys who worked on the first atom bomb, I guess. Once you see that something is possible, you're damn well going to make it happen if you can.

After I gave Irv and Grace my shopping list they handed me one: a whole blood transfusion kit. Irv put the cash in my hand for the necessaries and I got everything at Chiron Medical Supplies near Middlesex Hospital. "We'll need it for when she comes out of the soup," said Grace.

When our preparations were complete there was nothing to do but Justine Two. Irv and Grace assured me that Justine One had been created by this procedure so we did the same thing with isolating the image, lasering it through the diffraction grating, printing the interference pattern, then reducing the pattern to its particles and putting the particles into the soup in the drum. "There's our suspension of disbelief," said Irv.

Grace said, "Please don't say, 'This is the moment of truth'."

"I'm not sure what kind of a moment it is," said Irv, "so I'm saying nothing." He handed Grace the 240-volt zapper we'd rigged up. "You do it," he said to her.

Grace closed her eyes and did it. There was a flash, a primordial electrical smell and somebody belched loudly. Then there she was rising out of the soup, all black-and-white in her sopping wet western clothes: Justine Two. "Jesus," she said, "where's my fucking horse? Am I supposed to walk to El Paso?" Then she stared wildly around and clambered out of the drum so violently that the three of us had to hold it to keep from spilling the primordial soup all over Grace's studio. As it was, there was a big puddle and Justine Two stepped into it, sat down, and belched. "All right," she said, "I don't see anybody I know, so what kind of party is this?"

"It's not a party," said Grace.

"Why are you talking funny?" said J Two.

"I'm English," said Grace. "You're in London."

"That's a crock of shit," said J Two. "There aren't any London locations in this picture."

"You're not in a picture now," said Irv. "This is reality."

"That'll be the day," said J Two, and she fainted and fell back into the puddle.

"I wonder if Istvan's Justine started out like this," said Grace.

"I wasn't there so I couldn't say," said Irv.

She was really an awful-looking thing in black-and-white, and when we got her out of her wet clothes it was even worse. "I forgot about clothes," said Grace. "We'll have to get her other things to wear. Underthings as well, tights, shoes, whatever."

"Then what?" said Irv.

"I don't know yet," said Grace. We'd been working for a couple of weeks to bring this creature into the world but Grace was looking at it, at her I should say, as if the whole thing was totally unexpected.

"Well," said Irv to Grace, "while you're thinking about it you know what we have to do."

"I know," said Grace, "and I'll go first. Bleed me, Artie."

"I don't want to take too much," I said. "Let's just get her into full color so we can see where we are with this." Mind you, while we were doing all this the rest of London was going on as usual. Some trains were running, some weren't. The streets were full of buses and cars and pedestrians, the pubs were full of drinkers, and we were putting blood into this thing that had climbed out of our suspension of disbelief. Great.

As J Two filled up with color I felt a little stirring of interest. She was a good-looking woman, you had to give her that. "Hello, honey," she said as she came round. "Why don't you get naked with me." She stuck out her tongue which was quite a long one and gave me the wettest kiss I'd ever had. She tasted like a swamp full of incontinent crocodiles. My head went round, the room tilted several different ways, and the wall opened up to let some huge hopping thing into the room. "Mmmmm!" said J Two. "Oh yes, gimme that old-time religion, do it, do it, do it."

"Are you talking to me or the huge hopping thing?" I said. "I don't usually tilt this much on the first date."

"Artie, try to come down a little if you can," said Grace. "Justine, you'll have to slow down if you want to hang out with us. We're actually a pretty quiet crowd."

"Oh yeah?" said J Two. "Who died and left you in charge, Grandma?"

"Watch your mouth," said Irv.

"Up yours, Grandad," said J Two.

The room was heaving around and the thing that had hopped out of the wall was making obscene gestures but I still couldn't see its face. Maybe I'm St Anthony, I thought. Is this a temptation?

25 🐸 Detective Inspector Hunter

3 FEBRUARY 2004. I don't read much poetry any more but there are some poems that I go back to. There's one by Yeats that's certainly short enough to stay in my memory but I never get it exactly right and I have to turn to the page in his *Collected Poems* where the bookmark is:

MEMORY

One had a lovely face,
And two or three had charm,
But charm and face were in vain
Because the mountain grass
Cannot but keep the form
Where the mountain hare has lain.

The form where the hare slept is emptiness in the shape of the hare. Last night I dreamt that Rose Harland came to my bed. I was lying on my side and she shaped herself to my back and pressed herself against me. In the dream I woke up and said, "What?"

"I'm sorry," she whispered, "I didn't mean to wake you, I only wanted to get warm."

"That's all right," I said as I woke up out of the dream. I put my hand where she'd been but her side of the bed was cold.

26 🐀 Istvan Fallok

23 JANUARY 2004. I went up to Golders Green out of curiosity; I wanted to see how Chauncey and Justine were getting on. I didn't phone ahead, I thought I'd just drop in and catch them unawares. Not knowing where I'd find an off-licence in Golders Green I bought a bottle of Glenfiddich at Nicolas in Berwick Street. I like the red Nicolas sign with its yellow lettering, it has spiritual uplift.

I was standing on the Northern Line platform at Tottenham Court Road when I noticed a rat down among the cables by the tracks. I remembered reading somewhere that in London you're never more than ten feet away from a rat. That's about how far I was from this one when it turned and looked at me. "You looking at me?" I said. It didn't say anything but its nose was twitching. Then it went back to its cable run. I did a few bars of rat music in my head. I hate their naked tails and their superior attitude, their behind-the-scenes cynicism. Cockroaches too – you can scrunch as many as you like but they're laughing because they know they'll win in the end.

Justine. What made Irv Goodman and Chauncey Lim and me suddenly fall in love with her? Love, shit. Irv is eighty-three and he's got no business falling in love. I'm sixty-five and Chauncey's only in his forties but all of us are old enough to know better. Irv started it. Almost at the end of his life and wanting something impossible he comes to me and flings down the gauntlet: "You can do it, Istvan."

When I first saw the interference pattern on the white card I thought, Well, yes, I *am* interfering. Maybe she wants to stop in the video, maybe she wants to stay dead. But I was hot for her and I wanted her alive and I was in charge. Now she was with Chauncey Lim and for the most part I was glad to have her off my hands. Maybe I was a little jealous. Dead people! I wonder what Lazarus did when he came out of the tomb. Must have had a hell of a thirst. Did he head for the nearest pub? If he did, they probably gave him plenty of room at the bar.

The train came and I found a seat by the doors. A woman sat down next to me but at Goodge Street she moved to another seat. Did I still smell of primordial soup? Or maybe I just looked crazy. Whatever. So many different faces in the Underground. Chinese, Japanese, Pakistani, Afro-Caribbean, Afro-African, and a few white American and English ones. All of them had necks, some exposed by open coats or jackets, others hidden. Faces staring into space, faces reading, faces looking inward at the stories inside them.

It's a long ride to Golders Green and I had to change at Camden Town to the Edgware train. Up the steps and across through a crush of faces and footsteps and down again to the other platform. There was an Edgware train with its doors open and in I went. Not very many people this time. Chalk Farm, Belsize Park, Hampstead. Hampstead Heath was where I once walked with Luise von Himmelbett. We sat on a bench high up on the Heath with a view of London down below us. There are ghosts of me all over this town.

When next I looked out of the window we were above ground, in a long gray stretch of railroad-yard looking things and wintry afternoon daylight. Then here came Golders Green station. The last time I'd been there was years ago when I needed some Jewish records from Jerusalem the Golden.

I went down the stairs and out into the winter sky (very high and open, with gold-tinted clouds) and the last part of the day. Brightly lit newsagents and snack shops led me out of the station into lights and traffic and crossings and railings and the Finchley Road. After the cramped closeness of Soho

it all seemed very wide and spread out and strange to me.
Elijah's Lucky Dragon was only a short walk from the station,
between Leverton and Sons Ltd, Independent Funeral Direc-
tors since 1789, and The Gate Lodge pub. I wouldn't have
minded dropping in for a quick one but The Gate Lodge
sounded like designer beers and careful drinkers and the pub
front was red with hanging plants and yellow outlines on the
panels and windows, all very charming. I don't like charming
and I don't like careful drinkers. I like pubs plain and dark and
old-fashioned with names like The Hand of Glory, The Spade
and Coffin and The Jolly Sandboys. With serious drinkers.
There was a bus stop nearby with dark huddles of people and
buses coming and going. In this cold northern twilight the
buses looked larger and redder than the ones in my part of
town.

The sign on Rosalie Chun's restaurant was a green neon
dragon wearing a yarmulke. The red neon lettering was that
Chu-Chin-Chow cuneiform they used in movie titles back in
the 1930s and it was still being used as recently as *The World
of Suzie Wong* in the 1950s.

I looked through the glass door and saw the chairs up on
the tables and a black man mopping the floor. I tapped on the
glass and he came to the door shaking his head. "*Shabbas,*" he
said. "We're closed."

"*You're* working," I said.

"I'm the *schwartzer,*" he said.

"Can you tell me where the Chuns live?" I asked him.

"Why?"

"I'm a friend of Chauncey Lim's, he's staying with them.
Justine Trimble too."

"Who are you?"

"Istvan Fallok."

"Wait here," he said, and disappeared. I turned around and

watched the traffic. There wasn't much. After about five minutes he came back. "OK," he said. "Go to the side entrance and ring the bell."

"You're very careful," I said. "Been having any trouble here?" He shook his head and went back to his mopping.

I went round and found two bells, one above the other. No names. It was a three-story building. I rang the bottom bell. "Yes?" said a man's voice.

I told him who I was and said I'd come to see Justine.

"Ring the other bell," he said.

This time Chauncey Lim answered. "What?" he said.

"It's me," I said, "Istvan."

He buzzed me in and I went up the stairs to the second floor. There was a mezuzah on the doorpost so I touched my fingers first to my lips, then to the little metal cylinder. When Chauncey opened the door he didn't seem very glad to see me. "Did you kiss the mezuzah?" he said.

"Of course," I said. "I'm a multicultural kind of goy. Why? Have you converted to Judaism?"

"No, but you needn't be flippant. When the Lord smote all the firstborn in the land of Egypt, he passed over the houses of the children of Israel where they'd smeared the blood of the Paschal lamb on the doorposts as instructed by Moses. The mezuzah is a reminder of that."

"Wow," I said. "Did you read that in a fortune cookie?"

"All right," said Chauncey, "you can make jokes all you like but blood is a serious thing."

"Tell me about it," I said.

"Hear, O Israel!" said a strange voice. There was a parrot in a large cage in a corner of the room.

"That's Elijah," said Chauncey. "He's a member of the Chun family."

"Handsome bird," I said. "African gray?"

"Tishbite," said Elijah. "First Kings, not dew nor rain."

"Rosalie does Bible readings with him," said Chauncey.

"My word," said Elijah.

"OK already," said Chauncey.

"Some of my best friends are *goyim*," said Elijah.

"Great," I said, "but I still wouldn't want my sister to marry a parrot."

"Why didn't you phone before coming?" said Chauncey. "Is everything all right?"

"Everything's fine," I said. "I just didn't want you to make any preparations." I gave him the whiskey.

"Thanks," he said. He turned his back on Elijah and lowered his voice. "Has H-U-N-T-E-R been around again?"

"Not yet. Where's Justine?"

"Napping. She sleeps a lot." He looked as if he might say more but didn't. He got two glasses and poured the Glenfiddich.

"*L'chaim*," said Elijah.

"Cheers," said Chauncey without much enthusiasm.

"Here's to romance," I said.

He laughed in a small way. "That's right: all you need is love."

"How is she?" I said. "Are you topping her up or is she hunting?"

"Neither. Rosalie's been feeding her kosher Chinese plus Golem broth and gosky patties Ba'al Shem Tov and she seems to be thriving on it – she's even put on a pound or two."

"Wonderful! And she's not losing color?"

"No, she's looking great."

"Phwoarr," said Elijah.

"When do I get to see her?" I said to Chauncey.

"She'll be out in a minute or two. Have you been around to my place at all?"

"Yes. Couple of messages on your door." I gave them to him.

"Customers wanting to know about their orders," he said. "I'll get back to work soon."

"And Justine? What's our next move with her?"

"Rosalie says she can stop here indefinitely. She and Justine have become great chums."

"What about Rosalie's husband? Does he mind Justine's being here indefinitely?"

"Lester Chun isn't at home very much," said Chauncey. "He travels a lot."

We sat there with our drinks not making much eye contact while I looked around the room.

"You looking at me?" said Elijah.

"No," I said, "just the room." White walls and only one picture, a Chagall lithograph with an elongated female nude slanting to the right while being admired by a standing-on-air black cock with an inner man. Perhaps a full moon up above, perhaps an Eiffel tower down below, a man's face at the base? Looking at the picture I began to hear klezmer music in my mind. I thought of Luise von Himmelbett whom I loved a long time ago. And was unfaithful to. And lost. Maybe loss is the main action of the universe and we're here because the universe wants us to experience it. So why did I bring Justine Trimble out of my primordial soup? And why was I a little jealous of Chauncey Lim? I looked at the kelim under my feet and the pattern didn't do anything, didn't move forward and back like the optical-illusion bathroom tiles of my childhood.

"Yo, Uncle Ish," said Justine as she came into the room. She looked great and gave me a hug and a kiss. Her breath stank and when she stepped back she looked a little wild, the way she did when she came home on the night she killed Rose Harland and had sex with two different men afterward. "Anything I can do for you?" she said. "Chauncey won't mind, will you, Chaunce?"

"I don't care a rat's arse either way," said Chauncey.

"Do it, Uncle Ish," said Elijah. "Do Justine."

"You don't sound like yourself," I said to Chauncey. "Are you all right?"

"Sure," he said. "'The lotus springs from the mud.'"

"What lotus are we talking about?" I said.

"I'll let you know when I find out," said Chauncey.

"I'm a Texas lotus that sprung out of the soup," said Justine. "How about it, Ish? You up for a little action?"

"*Pas ce soir*, Josephine," I said. "Have a drink."

"Don't mind if I do," she said. She got it down her neck pretty quickly. "Well, if nobody needs me here I might as well take a walk."

"Good idea," said Chauncey, "a little exercise always puts roses in your cheeks."

"I'm off then," she said. "See you both later."

Chauncey and I drank more whiskey. "What is it?" I said after a while.

"What is what?" he said.

"Come on, Chaunce," I said. "There's something bothering you."

"I'll tell you the truth," he said. "My falling in love with Justine was a delusion that came out of my wanting to take her away from you. That was how it started, then when we got into sharing her it seemed a really cool thing to do but now..."

"Now what?"

"I find Justine disgusting. The whole thing disgusts me. You got into it because Irving Goodman was obsessed with Justine from watching her old movies. You caught the obsession from him and you manufactured this creature that's committed murder so that now we have to keep looking over our shoulders. How long will it go on?"

"That's a good question," I said. "I wish I knew the answer."

27 🐸 Justine Two

30 JANUARY 2004. When I stuck my tongue in that guy's mouth it made him crazy but he liked it and his johnson stood up like a man. But he didn't want to go all the way and he started fighting me when I went for his neck. I was strong enough to take charge but I was feeling funny, I was having flashes of dark and wet and I wanted a strong male gripping me from behind while my eggs spilled out oh yes. Hold on, I said to myself, this is no place to spawn, you're a movie star. Walk, don't hop, you're as human as anybody else. Or almost.

This was in a kind of alley full of little shops that sold books, maps, prints, posters, antiques and so on. People coming and going while I leaned against a wall for a little while till I got myself straight. That was Cecil Court. When I came out of there I was in a big bright street full of cars and people: St Martin's Lane. There were cafés and coffee shops with people eating and drinking and I thought I might try that but I didn't have any money. So I kept going until I passed a place where people were going in and lining up for tickets and then a store with opera music coming out of it. Kept going till I came to a corner and turned into a dark street where I saw a man coming toward me. I did my fainting thing and when he caught me I gave him a big wet kiss and it flew him to the moon. This time I kept my mind on my work and when I got to his neck I bit him good and started a nice flow. Oh boy there's nothing like getting it the natural way, no tubes or technical stuff. I didn't empty him, just had a nice top-up and he was feeling good about it the whole time so we had a little poontang party in a doorway. He wasn't able to get out of a sitting position so I sat on his lap and that worked fine. His cap fell off and some people passing by dropped money in it. I also took a little from his wallet for expenses but I gave back the wallet and helped him zip up his pants, then I kissed him goodbye and left him sitting there smiling and shaking his head. When I was half-way back to the corner I heard him yell, "Oh my God!" but I didn't turn around. Maybe he was married and he felt guilty all of a sudden.

Then I did feel hungry for regular food so I went back to a café I'd passed earlier, Gaby's Deli in the Charing Cross Road near Leicester Square. I was picking up street names because when I didn't see signs I asked people where I was. Gaby's had a yellow awning that said HOT SALT BEEF, FALAFEL, SALADS. A sign by the door said LONDON'S BEST VEGETARIAN FALAFEL & SALAD IN PITTA. And above the awning the name in big silver three-dimensional letters with Est. 1965. The place looked busy and it smelled good when I opened the door so I went inside. I had a salt beef on rye and a bottle of beer. They didn't have Coors or Corona so I had Maccabee because I thought it might be a Scotch beer but there was Jewish lettering on the label. The salt beef was nothing special but the beer was good. It was warm in there and the place was full of everybody's smells. There were a lot of foreigners talking in their different languages. The lights were too bright and the voices were too loud. The man and woman at the table behind me, maybe they thought they weren't talking loud. He was saying in his English accent, "There's no reason to fake it if you can't come, you don't have to put on a performance for me." "I wasn't faking it," she lied. Jesus, the things these people worry about. Where I come from the women don't have time to fake it because the men are all done in ten seconds or less. But Gaby's was OK – people talking and laughing and a couple of men giving me the eye. Well, I thought, it's a long hop from El Paso but London isn't so bad.

There must have been a couple of pounds of salt beef in

my sandwich and I was still working on it with my second Maccabee when this guy comes in and sits down facing me. Worn-out looking character in his sixties, white hair but he might have been a redhead once. "Justine!" he says.

"How come you know my name?" I said.

"What is this," he said, "amnesia? I brought you into the world, for Christ's sake."

"In a pig's ass you did," I said.

"Why aren't you in Golders Green?" he said. "You're looking a little strange too. Are you on something?"

"Look, Buster," I said, "I don't know what you're talking about or how you got my name but if you're coming on to me I have to tell you that this salt beef and the beer are really weighing me down and I don't feel much like spawning right now."

"Spawning!" he said. "What are you, a salmon?"

"Not quite," I said. "You wanna see my warts?"

"Some other time," he said. "I don't know what you're on but you're a little bit too weird for me tonight. I'll see you around."

"Not if I see you first," I told him. When he left I was remembering his scrawny white neck. The salt beef and the beer were going round and round in me so I paid up and just made it outside in time to barf in the street which didn't get me any applause from the passers-by. I went back to Cecil Court hoping to find somebody to take the bad taste out of my mouth and there was Mr Scrawny from Gaby's looking in the window of a bookstore. "Oh," he said, "it's you" when I tapped him on the shoulder.

"Sorry I wasn't more friendly back there in Gaby's Deli," I said. "Let me make it up to you."

"No problem," he said, "but I'll take a rain check if that's all right with you."

"Well, friend," I said, "it ain't, so I'll just have a little taste of your neck if you don't mind."

"But I *do* mind," he said, too late because I already had my teeth in him. "Well," he said just before he passed out, "this'll teach me to let Irv Goodman give me a bottle of Scotch."

I was still trying to get a good flow going when I realized he was empty. I guess these old ones run dry pretty quick.

gone. I don't know what came over me. Look, I don't want to be wasting your time so I really should be going."

"Don't go just yet," I said. "It's been my experience that these huge hopping things don't usually turn up without a reason. Two beers wouldn't do it. Was there anything before the hopping thing?"

"Ah! The woman. . ."

"What woman?"

"Standing next to me. Suddenly she crumpled and I caught her just before she hit the ground. I said, 'Gotcha' and she held on to me. She gave me a great big wet slobbery kiss. My God, she tasted awful, then she was nuzzling my neck. Her mouth was very wet and she began to bite me but I fought her off."

"Then what?"

"Then she wasn't there but the hopping thing came after me – didn't attack me, just kept hopping behind me with a squelching sound each time it hit the ground."

"Can you describe the woman?"

"Quite pretty, blond, about five foot six. Her clothes were damp and smelly."

"What was she wearing?"

"Some kind of western outfit. Cowboy boots."

"Do you mind if I take a swab from your mouth and your neck?" I said.

"What for?" he said.

"You never know," I said. Afterward I took his address and phone number and gave him my card. "Let me know if you remember anything else," I said. "Any time of the day or night." I sent the samples off to the lab and that was it for Monday evening. When I got home I took my shoes off, put my feet up, drank some whiskey, and listened to Alison Krauss and the Cox family. I fell asleep in my chair and dreamt that

Rose Harland was waiting for me on the far-side bank of Jordan. "I'll be waiting, drawing pictures in the sand," she sang, "and when I see you coming I will rise up with a shout. And come running through the shallow waters, reaching for your hand." I could still see her face as I woke up, then it faded and I went to bed. As I was drifting off to sleep I heard myself say, "Definitely not a mouse turd."

1 February 2004. Scotland Yard e-mailed me a photo sent by Ralph Darling of Witheridge in Devon. He'd written to say that his sister Rachael had gone to London last November in a depressed state of mind and he hadn't heard from her since. He was worried about her and he wanted to know if there was any news of her. A living face in a photograph looks quite different to a dead one but when I had the Devon photo side by side with ours I was pretty sure it was a match. So that was her name, Rachael Darling. I rang up Ralph Darling and he came in to identify the body of his sister.

He was a very large man in corduroy trousers and a reefer jacket. I'm six feet tall and he was half a head taller and broad. He had big hands, rough and red, and he smelled of cows. "It never goes away," he said. "I've got an organic dairy farm outside Witheridge."

Rachael was in the mortuary at St Hubert's Hospital. I took her brother there and sat him down in the little waiting room while I went through to talk to Morton Taylor, the technician. Taylor consulted his clipboard and wheeled a trolley over to the banks of refrigerated body trays. He raised the trolley bed up to No. 12 and slid Rachael Darling's tray on to it. Then he transferred her to another trolley with a blue floral-print skirt, put a pillow under her head and a blanket over her, and wheeled her into the chapel of rest where the lighting is subdued so the paleness of death won't be too startling and the atmosphere seems hushed by virtue of a large wooden cross on a stand. I always expect a recording of non-denominational organ music, "Tales from the Vienna Woods" or whatever and I'm always thankful for its absence.

At this point I brought Ralph Darling in. He came over to the bier, looked down at her, sobbed and covered his face with his hands. After a few moments he took his hands away. "That's her," he said, and clenched his fists. "She looks so pale, like a ghost. How'd she die?"

"We can't know for certain," I said.

"I think you *do* know. Don't play games with me."

"All right, but you won't like it."

"Go on, Inspector."

"All the blood was drained out of her body," I said.

He was becoming very angry, I thought he was going to hit me and he was about twenty-eight pounds heavier than I was. "How?" he said. "Who did it?"

I pointed to the wound in her neck.

"What?" he said. "Is this some kind of horrible joke? Are you telling me there are vampires in London?"

"I've told you all I know," I said. "I'm sorry."

He stood there shaking his head for a while. "Could I have a look at her flat?" he said.

I took him round to Beak Street. On the way there I said, "Was she married?"

"No," he said.

"Anyone in her life, a boyfriend?"

"No, why are you asking?"

"When a case is still unsolved like this I try to find out as much as I can," I said. When we got to the flat I removed the police tapes from the door, and we went inside. He stood there taking in the goneness of his sister. London silences always have the background of London traffic. "Could I be alone in here for a few minutes?" he said.

"Certainly, I'll wait for you outside."

After about ten minutes he came out. "Do you think you'll find whoever did this?" he said.

"We have a suspect that we want to talk to," I said, "but that's all I can tell you just now."

"I understand," he said. "Thank you." We shook hands and he walked away slowly.

30 🐗 Dr. Wilbur Flood

31 JANUARY 2004. I was coming through Cecil Court early in the morning on my way to the lab when I heard a woman singing with a down-home accent:

> Tweedle-O-Twill, puffin' on corn silk,
> Tweedle-O-Twill, whittlin' wood,
> Settin' there wishin' he could go fishin'
> Over the hill, Tweedle-O-Twill.

That's a Gene Autry song, and the last time I heard it was back in Tennessee about thirty years ago. My daddy used to sing it when he was working on his old Ford pickup.

She was sitting in a doorway with a man slumped against her. I noticed that she was wearing cowboy boots. She didn't look homeless and neither did the man. I stopped in front of them and she said, "Howdy."

"Howdy," I said. "Been having a late night?"

"I been saving the last dance for you," she said. "Whyn't you come a little closer, honey."

It's hard to say no to a good-looking woman even if she seems a little the worse for wear. "Won't your friend mind?" I said.

"It don't make no never-mind to him," she said. "He's dead to the world." She reached up and pulled me down to her and gave me a big wet slobbery kiss with her tongue half-way down my throat. She tasted like my high-school friend Barbara-Ann Hopper only ten times worse. Oh my God, I thought – a toad-sucker in London! Then she was trying to bite my neck but I got loose and backed away as fast as I could. Everything was going round and round with the ground sometimes tilting up and sometimes down while out of the corner of my eye I saw some great big hopping thing coming after me. I sprinted down Cecil Court, dodged through the traffic in St Martin's Lane with the thing close behind, made a sharp right towards the Coliseum, then left and left again and so on trying to lose it but when I reached the lab it was still hot on my heels. Once I got inside I phoned the police while the hopping thing did its best to come through the wall. Scared? I didn't know whether to shit or go blind so I just kind of closed one eye and farted and hoped for better times. It took about an hour and a whole lot of black coffee before the thing left off thumping and squelching and went back to wherever it lives.

When PC Plod got to Cecil Court Miss Tweedle-O-Twill was long gone but her friend was still there. He was dead to the world all right, stone dead with all the blood sucked out of him.

31 🐀 Medical Examiner
Harrison Burke

31 JANUARY 2004. When Wilbur had drunk nine or ten cups of black coffee and was more or less back to normal we looked at the lab report on Walter Dixon. Wilbur, who's from Tennessee, said, "I don't need this report to tell me that what we got here is a toad-sucker."

"A what?" I said.

His answer was part of a poem:

> How about them toad-suckers,
> Ain't they clods?
> Sittin' there suckin'
> Them green toady-frogs.

"Toad-suckers," I said. "Have you ever seen one before this?"

"I dated one when I was in high school," he said: "Barbara-Ann Hopper. She hung out with a crowd of older boys and they used to kid her about her name. They said she ought to try tripping with one of her relatives. So she did and she liked the effect. She said that sucking those little warty ones made her horny."

"Did you ever try it, Wilbur?" I asked him.

"No, but I tried *her* shortly after she had one."

"And?"

"I didn't care for the taste but I'd rate her eleven out of ten for the rest of it."

"Bufotoxin," I read from the report. "Walter Dixon's saliva shows traces of bufotoxin. Where would a toad-sucker find a toad in London? You can get frog's legs in a French restaurant but as far as I know there's no pub where you can step up to the bar and ask for a little warty guy. You know of any?"

"No, I don't," said Wilbur, "but that woman who snogged me sure as hell had a toad connection."

"A toad pusher?" I said. "You never know – London seems to be full of surprises these days."

32 🐸 Detective Inspector Hunter

31 JANUARY 2004. When I saw the body I rang Burke on my mobile. "Istvan Fallok's on his way to you," I said. "Running on empty."

"Fallok!" said Burke. "I'd heard about Cecil Court from Wilbur but I didn't know who the victim was. He's still shaking from the bufotoxin snogging and the great big hopping thing."

"I'll be over as soon as I finish with the crime scene," I said. "Don't go away."

"I'm not going anywhere. Wilbur just went out for a six-pack."

"This one's really hitting you hard, is it."

"Definitely worth getting out of bed for. See you."

When I got to the lab I went through the door marked No Entry – Protective Clothing Must Be Worn In This Area and walked into the post-mortem smell which is partly butcher shop, partly fecal matter, and partly Hycolin disinfectant. Burke and Wilbur in their blue lab gowns, plastic aprons and wellies were standing by a white dissecting table on which lay Istvan Fallok, being considerably more open than when last we spoke, in fact he no longer had any secrets whatever. Except, of course, the identity of his killer.

I joined my colleagues as they went on with their work in the quiet hiss of fresh air coming in from the blower. Wilbur recorded the contents of Fallok's stomach and weighed it while Burke busied himself with the rib shears and I averted my eyes. "Salt beef on rye," said Wilbur. "This says surprise attack to me; if he'd known it was to be his last nosh he'd have had something better."

"I love it when you talk forensic," I said, "but what about a suspect?"

"Are you kidding?" said Wilbur. "The DNA from the saliva on Fallok's neck and jacket is the same as the DNA from the saliva on Walter Dixon's neck and jacket, and Dixon also got snogged in Cecil Court. And if you take a sample from my neck and jacket you'll get more of the same from that bufotoxiniferous cutie who stuck her tongue down *my* throat: Miss Tweedle-O-Twill."

"Tweedle-O-Twill?" I said.

"That's a Gene Autry song," Burke explained.

"And she was wearing cowboy boots," said Wilbur.

"Blond," I said, "pretty, about five foot six, good figure?"

"That's her," said Wilbur.

"Sounds like Justine Trimble," I said. "When we took a sample of her saliva from Rose Harland's neck the DNA was the same as Fallok's. We took samples from Fallok, Lim, Goodman and Justine. The sample just taken from Fallok doesn't match any of those if my notes are correct."

"Right," said Burke.

"So what have we got here?" I said: "Two Justines? What, are they cloning her now?"

"Vampires move with the times like everyone else," said Wilbur. "Anyone for a beer?"

"Are you enjoying this?" I said to him.

"Yes," he said. "I get tired of the same old thing day after day."

"So do I," I said, "but you get your kicks in this nice clean air-conditioned lab while I wear myself out catching the villains and villainesses."

"If you'd had better A Levels you might have got into medical school and then maybe you'd be working in a lab too," said Wilbur.

"Careful," I said. "The next big hopping thing that comes after you might be me."

Wilbur got quiet then and concentrated on his work. I think his bufotoxin trip was still fresh in his mind. As for me, I had to tear myself away and go looking for new dots to connect.

33 🦫 Grace Kowalski

31 JANUARY 2004. The doorbell woke me a little after nine in the morning. Irv was still asleep and snoring peacefully. "Who is it?" I said over the intercom.

"Well, it ain't Little Joe the wrangler," said J Two.

Afraid to think of what she might have been doing since she went out last night, I went down to let her in. She looked a mess and there were spatters of blood all down the front of her. "They got the gold," she said.

"I was too late to stop them. Where's my horse?"

"You haven't got a horse," I said. "You're not in a film now, you're in London."

"All right," she said. "How come he knew my name?"

Irv was with us by then. "Who?" he said. "Who knew your name?"

"The old guy who came on to me in Gaby's Deli."

"What'd he say to you?" I asked her.

"He talked crazy, said he'd brought me into the world and wanted to know why I wasn't in Geldings Green."

"Golders Green? Oh my God," I said, "that was Istvan. What happened then?"

"Nothing right then, only after I threw up I didn't feel so good and when I saw his neck I went for it. How the hell was I to know?"

"Know what?" said Irv.

"That he'd run dry so soon. I never meant to empty him."

"You killed him?" I said.

"I guess you could say that – he passed out while I was still trying to get a little nourishment out of him and that's all she wrote."

"Oh God," I said, "it's all my fault. I wanted to teach him a lesson and this is what I did."

"You didn't do it alone," said Irv. "I was in it with you from the beginning, and before that I was the one who got Istvan into this whole Justine thing, so I'm guiltier than you are. If I hadn't gone to his place with a bottle of Bowmore Cask Strength Islay Malt he might be alive today."

"His last words," said J Two, "were, 'That'll teach me to let Irv Goodman give me a bottle of Scotch.'"

"Thank you," said Irv. "How wonderful to have his last words to cherish."

"OK," I said, "we did a bad thing but beating ourselves up about it isn't going to bring Istvan back. Maybe we can move on to doing a good thing."

"Like what?" said Irv.

"I don't know," I said. J Two had fallen asleep in a chair and was snoring loudly. We were both looking at her and our eyes met.

"Well," said Irv. "That's why they put erasers on pencils, isn't it."

34 🦫 Detective Inspector Hunter

31 JANUARY 2004. We hadn't been around to Hermes Sound-ways since Fallok's death, so that was where PS Locke and I went next. Bingo, there were two people inside, Irving Good-man and a woman whom I hadn't seen before. When Locke knocked they had to open, and when I'd identified myself to the woman I said, "Now then, who are you?"

"Grace Kowalski," she said.

"Do you know anything about the death of Istvan Fallok?" I said.

"I think I do," she said. Goodman just stood there shaking his head and looking miserable.

"You *think* you do," I said to Kowalski. "Discuss."

"We were told about Istvan's death by the one who appar-ently caused it."

"*Apparently?*" I said. "*Who* apparently?"

"Justine. . ." she said.

"Two," said Goodman.

"Justine too?" I said. "Justine also?"

"Justine Number Two," said Kowalski.

"Are you telling me there are two Justines?" I said. "Are they twins?"

"Not born that way," said Goodman.

"I see," I said, "they weren't born as twins but they became twins later in life. If I had the time to be amused I'd probably find the two of you strangely entertaining, but I haven't the time, and unless you both start talking straight you're going to be in a whole lot of trouble. Now, on my com-mand: Speak!"

"You won't believe us," said Kowalski. "What we're going to tell you sounds impossible."

"In my line of work I sometimes have to believe six impossible things before breakfast," I said. "Stop stalling and start talking."

"Both Justines were reconstituted from the magnetic particles of a videotape," said Goodman. He stopped and waited for me to say something.

"Wonderful," I said. "Carry on."

"Once the particles were in a suspension of disbelief," said Kowalski, "ingredients were added to make a primordial soup which was then zapped with 240 volts of electricity to precipitate the whole flesh-and-blood person."

"Is that it?" I said.

"Briefly," said Goodman. "If we get technical it's a long story."

"I don't doubt it," I said. "We can return to this later, but at the moment I'm more interested in Justine Two's whereabouts."

"We don't know," said Kowalski. "We were going to. . ."

"Restrain her but she's very violent," said Goodman. "She chased us out of Grace's place which is why we came here."

"I think she's probably left there by now," said Kowalski.

"Where is your place?" I said.

"In Berwick Street," she said. So we went and checked out All That Glisters and the studio flat over it and came up empty.

"Well," I said to Goodman and Kowalski, "so much for where she isn't. Now that you've had a little time to think about your story, can you improve on the last version?"

"You didn't believe us, did you?" said Goodman.

"Did you expect me to?" I said.

"What about your six impossible things before breakfast?" said Kowalski.

107

"I was talking about *believable* impossible things," I said. "Now, have you anything useful to say about Justine Two?"

"We've told you all we know," said Goodman.

"Right," I said. "Very good." To PS Locke I said, "Book them for perverting the course of justice and hindering a police investigation."

"OK, Guv," said Locke. He read them their rights, cuffed them, and took them to the nick. It wasn't much but it was the only way I could relieve my feelings.

35 🐸 Irving Goodman

1 FEBRUARY 2004. Handcuffs for God's sake. As if we were violent people. Our arms were crossed with the cuffed wrists spaced apart by a thick plastic bar so that even if I'd had the key in one hand I'd not have been able to use it. Any movement caused pain but when I asked Sergeant Locke to loosen the cuffs he said no. PC Fast pushed our heads down in the regulation manner as we got into the back of an unmarked police car and off we went through Saturday evening streets where Londoners not in handcuffs were starting the weekend in their various ways.

At the police station we went round to the trade entrance and were driven through barred gates to the custody suite. We were taken through a heavy steel gate to the reception area where the custody sergeant sat behind a long counter. It was still early in the evening but the place had an all-night feel and the voices and footsteps were the sound of what is always waiting behind the paper-thin façade of everyday.

PS Locke told the custody sergeant why we'd been arrested, we were booked in, searched, and the contents of our pockets put in evidence bags. Our shoelaces and belts were also taken from us. Grace and I both told the custody sergeant that we couldn't tell them anything they'd believe and that was duly noted. Our rights and entitlements were read to us and I used my phone call to ring up Artie. "Uncle Irv!" he said, "Are you OK?"

"No problem," I said. "I just wanted you to know where we are." Grace didn't phone anyone. We were questioned about our health and although my chest was feeling pretty dodgy I didn't ask to be seen by a doctor; I refused to give them the satisfaction.

After being fingerprinted and photographed we were taken to adjoining cells. Mine had a stale smell as if the air hadn't been changed for a long time. The door was a solid metal thing with a pass-through slot called a wicket. Next to it was a spyhole. The walls were tiled, the bed was a bench with a thin blue-covered mattress, blue blankets and pillow, and there was a toilet. We were given a cup of tea and something out of a microwave. It tasted brown but I don't know what it was. When I lay down on the bed I saw, high above me, a printed message on the ceiling:

CRIMESTOPPERS 0800 555 111
Anonymous information about
crime could earn a cash reward

"Look, Ma," I said. "Top of the world."

I tapped on the wall but got no response so I guessed it was too thick. I went to the door, put my mouth close to the wicket, and said, "Grace?" No answer. "Grace," I shouted, "can you hear me?"

"Yes," she shouted back, "I can hear you."

"Well," I said, "one thing leads to another, doesn't it. You start reconstituting dead movie stars and this is where you end up."

"I still can't believe that I caused Istvan's death," she said. "That'll always be with me, it'll never go away."

"Everything goes away after a while," I said. "This whole thing started with me. Don't ask me to explain how I got fixated on Justine Trimble because I can't. It must have been some kind of senile dementia."

"Three more or less intelligent men," said Grace, "all with the hots for a woman who died forty-seven years ago."

"Weird shit happens," I said.

"You think you're over that by now?"

"I've told you, Grace, that particular folly's behind me."

"Not beside you? Not *in*side you?"

"Nope. All gone."

"I'm pretty tired," said Grace. "I think I'll try to get some sleep."

"Me too. Goodnight, Grace."

"Night, Irv. See you later."

I kept my clothes on and covered myself with both blankets but I still couldn't get warm. I thought of old King David, how he gat no heat even when they put Abishag the Shunammite in his bed. Grace would have made me warm. Eventually I fell asleep but I kept dreaming and half waking and falling back into the same dream.

In this dream I was Captain Bligh at the tiller of the *Bounty*'s launch, watching the ship sail away with the mutineers as they threw video cassettes overboard. No, not the *Bounty*: the name I read on the stern was *Body*. "Wait a minute," I said in the dream, "I'm not Captain Bligh. What's this mutiny all about? The crew were always perfectly willing to take my orders. Where am I supposed to go with this boat?"

"They've given you a sextant and a compass," said Fallok, "and there's no better navigator than you, Captain." How can I suspend my disbelief? I thought. He has such confidence in me as HMS *Body* sails away and leaves me in command of this overloaded vessel that must face seas too big for it. Smaller and smaller in the distance grows the ship that is no longer mine. And down, down, down goes Justine in the fathomless deep, flickering on the screen of the ocean mind, riding, riding, riding to the blackness and the stillness below the flickering.

I came all the way awake and went to where I'd stood to talk to Grace. "Irv?" she shouted.

"I'm here," I shouted back.

"I woke up," she said.

"Yes, Grace?"

"I'm an alone kind of person, really. . ." she said.

"Me too," I said.

"I was wondering. . ." she said.

"Wondering what?"

"Nothing, really."

"Tell me, Grace, go on."

"You tell me what you think I was wondering, OK?"

"OK. You were wondering about me?"

"Yes. Don't stop."

"Wondering how I feel about you?"

"Yes."

"Grace, when I think about you and me I remind myself that I'm eighty-three years old and I haven't got a whole lot of future in front of me."

"Maybe whatever there is is enough, Irv, if. . ."

"If there's love?"

"Yes."

"Are you waiting for me to say something?"

"I think so."

"Fnerg," said Inner Irv.

"I didn't catch that," said Grace.

"Come on, Grace – I'm too old for this kind of thing."

"The question you have to ask yourself," she said, "is, 'Do I feel dead?'"

"Well, no."

"Prove it."

"Grace," I shouted, "I love you, OK?"

"I love you too, Irv. Well, goodnight then."

"Goodnight, Grace." We both (she told me later) kissed the air in front of us and went back to sleep.

36 🐀 Chauncey Lim

2 FEBRUARY 2004. I knew I'd have to start catching up with
my business and I thought I might as well begin on this quiet
Monday. I made myself a sandwich lunch, then on my way
out I went into the restaurant where Justine was eating latkes
Liu Hai.

"Enjoying your lunch?" I said.

For a moment she seemed not to recognise me. "Sure," she
said. "I'm home on the Jewish-Chinese range."

"I'm off to my place to see what needs doing," I said. "I'll
see you later."

"See you," she said.

As I was leaving I saw Charles, the black man who works
at the restaurant. "You know," he said, "there've been a lot of
dead rats lately."

"Why tell me about it?" I said.

"Just sharing the local news," he said. "They've all had
their heads bitten off. And no blood in them."

"Thanks for sharing," I said. "Mind how you go."

"You too," he said.

It's a long slow trip from Golders Green back to town.
Some of the people on the train seemed to be staring at me
and I tried not to notice but found myself wondering if I'd
become someone to be stared at; I knew that I was no longer
the Chauncey I used to be before I took up with Justine. My
disgust had become depression and my thoughts were dreary.
Some things that can be done are better left undone, and Justine was one of them.

I got off at Tottenham Court Road and walked to D'Arblay

Street. There were not many people about in that part of Soho and the streets were full of emptiness. When I got to Chauncey Lim, Photographic Novelties, the place seemed small and from another time, as if I'd come back to the house of my childhood. There were a couple of notes stuck to the door and inside there were some letters on the floor. From Everything for the Office in Bangkok there was an invoice for a gross of Whoopee Spinners, and from Educational Products in Akron, Ohio, a check for a gross of After-School Pencil Peepshows. The others were from people who wanted to know what had happened to their orders. The place smelled stale, my photographic novelties were rubbish, and the acupuncture chart and Aunt Zophrania's calendar on the wall looked stupid.

I wrote a check for Everything for the Office, locked up, posted the check to Bangkok, and went on to Berwick Street and All That Glisters. Grace was alone, drinking vodka and looking terrible. "What's the matter?" I said.

"Haven't you heard about Istvan?" she said.

"No. What happened?"

"He's dead."

It wasn't as if we'd ever been that close, but Fallok's death knocked me sideways. I sat down suddenly and Grace gave me all the details while I listened and shook my head in disbelief. "It was J Two that finished him," she said. "I told Inspector Hunter but he wouldn't believe me."

"Two Justines!" I said. 'Whose idea was that?'

"Mine," she said. "Irv and I did it together with Irv's nephew Artie. Artie did most of the work, actually."

"Where's J Two now?"

"Nobody knows."

"And Irv?"

"He's in hospital."

"What happened to him?"

"He came down with double bronchial pneumonia after we spent a night in the nick."

"You were locked up?"

"That's right."

"What for?"

"As I said, Hunter wouldn't believe us when we told him about J Two and he got pissed off so he nicked us."

"Of course he wouldn't believe it, Grace. I shouldn't have gone up to Golders Green. What you needed around here was a voice of reason."

"Whatever. I can't get over it that Istvan's dead because of me."

" 'If you can't get over it you must get over it anyway.' Wise words from a famous teacher, Grace."

"Confucius?"

"No, Rabbi Yisakhar Baer of Radoshitz."

"Those famous rabbis could sit around being wise because their wives did all the work. Wisdom is foolishness and foolishness is wisdom in my book. What are your plans now?"

"I'm waiting for word from Elijah."

"The prophet Elijah?"

"That's the one."

"How's he going to contact you?"

"In a dream, I expect. That's how he did it last time."

"Lucky you. When you see him, maybe you could tell him I'd be grateful for advice if he's in the neighborhood."

"OK. What're you going to do now?"

"Finish this bottle. Would you like to help me?"

"Yes, thanks. That's the best offer I've had today." So we sat there drinking and shaking our heads. Grace put on some music to help us along: Johnny Cash, *The Man in Black*. She started the CD on "Sunday Morning Coming Down". We were well into Monday afternoon but that was the right song for the occasion.

By now I was feeling that wherever I was, I should be somewhere else. Trouble seemed to be waiting for me round every corner but if I didn't go back to Golders Green I was afraid Golders Green would come looking for me. So I went. While I was standing on the platform at Tottenham Court Road I saw a rat down among the cables by the tracks. It was looking up at the platform, and when it saw me it seemed to take fright and scurried back the way it had come.

The train was half empty; stations came and went as it plodded northward and it emerged aboveground as the sun was setting in the full dreariness of Monday evening. When I got to Elijah's Lucky Dragon I went right up to the flat. Justine was nowhere to be seen. Elijah greeted me with "How're they hangin', Chaunce?"

"Don't be familiar," I said.

"Just a closer walk with thee," said Elijah. "Put on your red dress, baby, cause we're goin' out tonight." He's acquired an odd repertoire of gospel and blues from Charles and he was starting the next verse when the doorbell rang.

"Who is it?" I said.

"Detective Inspector Hunter," said the intercom. "May I come up?"

"Come ahead," I said, and buzzed him in. When I opened the door there were DI Hunter and a sharp-looking black woman. I'd seen her in the Underground but hadn't realized she was following me.

"This is Detective Patterson," said Hunter.

"Sure," I said. "Why not?"

"Where's Justine Trimble?" said Hunter.

"No idea," I said.

"There is a balm in Gilead," said Elijah.

"That's a hymn," said Hunter.

"That's a her too," said Elijah.

"Where?" said Hunter.

"Rice and beans, flour and potatoes," said Elijah.

"In the storeroom?" said Hunter.

"Heal a sin-sick soul," said Elijah.

"Where does this parrot get his material?" said Hunter.

"He hangs out with Charles," I said.

"Who's Charles?"

"Black man who works here."

"In the storeroom?"

"Wherever he's needed," I said.

"Like Mars bars," said Elijah.

"What's he talking about?" said Hunter to me.

"No idea," I lied.

Hunter fixed me with a very beady eye. "Right," he said. "Let's visit the storeroom."

We had to go through the restaurant and there we encountered Rosalie Chun. "So," she said, looking at Hunter and Detective Patterson, "who are you and what do you want?"

Hunter and Patterson identified themselves and showed their warrant cards. "We're just having a look around," said Hunter.

"What are you looking for?" said Rosalie.

"We'll know it when we find it," said Hunter. "We'll try the storeroom first."

"No violations here," said Rosalie. "I run a clean restaurant."

"I'm sure you do," said Hunter. "Would you like to lead the way?"

We all went down to the storeroom and there was Justine with blood all around her mouth and a headless rat in her right hand like a Mars bar. Before you could say Jackie Chan she threw the rat straight at DI Hunter. He ducked and it hit Detective Patterson in the face. While Patterson screamed and flailed about Justine scooped up a double handful of rice

from a sack and flung it in our eyes. In the moment this gave
her she went through us as if she'd been shot from a cannon
and was up the stairs and gone.

"*Gevalt!*" said Rosalie. "After all the wonderful meals I've
made for her!"

"You can't expect gratitude from her kind," said Hunter.

"Is that a racist remark?" I said. I couldn't help it.

"Don't you cheek me, sunshine," said Hunter. "You're nicked
for perverting the course of justice and hindering a police
investigation. Read him his rights, Detective Patterson."

Still wiping blood from her face, Patterson said to me, "You
have the rat to remain silent, right. But anything you do say
will be bitten off in evidence and taken down against you."
With that we all left Elijah's Lucky Dragon and that was it
for Monday.

37 🐿 Irving Goodman

2 FEBRUARY 2004. During the night it blew a gale and the seas were running very high. In the morning wind and sea abated and I was going to give each man a teaspoonful of rum and a quarter breadfruit and a coconut but it was difficult to see anyone. A voice spoke up and said, "You are not Captain Bligh, Sir. You are not even Sir."

I hate it when dreams become difficult. "Give me a break," I said. "I'm doing the best I can and I intend to sail this boat all the way to the Thames Estuary and Knock John." As the fog cleared the old fort came into view and I heard Charlotte saying, "Here on Britain's Better Music Station the time is coming up to what it used to be and Jo Stafford has a song for all you haunted hearts out there."

> In the night, though we're apart,
> There's a ghost of you within my haunted heart –
> Ghost of you, my lost romance,
> Lips that laugh, eyes that dance. . .

"Charlie," I said, "is that you?"
"Of course it is," she said, "always."

38 🐀 Justine Trimble

3 FEBRUARY 2004. That son of a bitch Chauncey, he couldn't leave well enough alone, he had to sick the police on me. What the hell was his beef? I was giving him as much white pussy as he could handle. So I was doing rats, big deal. Did he think I could live on that Jew–Chinese cooking and nothing else? I didn't ask to be brought back from the dead and I'm sick and tired of being hounded by everybody and his brother. They made me a vampire and I do what vampires do. If they wanted Shirley Temple they should have used a different recipe.

I never meant to kill Rose Harland, she was the only sweet thing that's happened to me since I became undead. I remember the softness of her lips and how she clung to me while I held her to keep her from falling.

There's no sweetness for me any more. That fucking Chauncey.

39 🐗 Ralph Darling

4 FEBRUARY 2004. The emptiness left by Rachael's death was bigger than whatever else there was around it. All those years of her gone! After I saw Detective Inspector Hunter I went home and arranged for my foreman to run the farm for me, then I booked a room for two weeks at the Regent Palace Hotel near Piccadilly Circus. Every morning I woke up and looked out of my window at a row of orange wheelie bins with a row of scooters and motorbikes in front of them in Glasshouse Street. Eros was not part of my view. Every day I walked up Brewer Street to Lexington near the corner of Beak, the spot where Hunter thought Rachael had been killed. I had a feeling that the person or thing that had killed her might return to it. I knew that Rachael was with me and I sensed that I could tune into her killer through her.

People came and went. Day after day and night after night nothing happened until yesterday evening. The dark came early and the street lamps didn't so much illuminate as just give everything a yellowish cast. I could feel a lurking presence – I could almost see a dim shape as if I were wearing night-vision goggles. Whatever it was was coming closer. I had no weapon but there was a skip full of rubbish and I saw the legs of a wooden chair sticking out of it. I broke off a chair leg and waited. Somebody got between me and the dim shape and I said, "Get out of the way!" but he didn't, and it was on him. Everything went into slow motion then, I couldn't see very well and it took me a long time to get to where it was happening. I saw it clearly then, a young woman bending over the man on the ground. She had her teeth in his neck and she looked up at me with blood running down her chin.

It was like a Hammer horror film. I knocked her away from the man with the chair leg, then I grabbed her by the hair and jammed the chair leg into what I hoped was her heart. She let out a terrible scream and a geyser of blood shot up out of her. Then she became black-and-white, then flat, then nothing but dust blowing in the wind. There was no blood on the pavement. The chair leg was lying there but she was gone and the man was dead. He was Chinese.

"Was that the one that killed you?" I said to Rachael, and I felt a heaviness go away from me so I knew I'd got it right. I walked back through the noise and dirt of London to the Regent Palace Hotel and in the morning I checked out and went home.

40 🐗 Detective Inspector Hunter

3 FEBRUARY 2004. "Shall we put the score at Vampires three, Plod nil?" said Burke.

"A true Briton would not support Vampires," I said.

"Who said I was supporting them?" said Burke. "I'm just telling it like it is. Here's poor old Chauncey Lim missing all of his blood and found in the neighborhood of our usual suspects. That makes a hat-trick for the other side. Have you got a clue?"

"You can be very irritating at times, Harry."

"I've been told that before," said Burke. "I can't think why. Have you got a suspect?"

"Well, there are two Justines out there now and my money's on Justine One."

"I suppose you've got a fifty-fifty chance of being right. What's your next move?"

"That's on a need-to-know basis, Harry."

"Oh, yes. Who needs to know?"

"I do."

I looked at Chauncey Lim's dead face, at his bloodless body, at what remained of whatever he was and whatever he wanted and hoped for. All of that had been drained out of him with the blood and now he was something small and left behind. Might he still be alive if I'd kept him in the nick another day? Probably she'd have got him sooner or later now that she'd come out. There was a tattoo on his chest, a line of Chinese characters. There were no relatives in this country so Rosalie and Lester Chun came to view the body and Lester was kind enough to translate the tattoo. "Form, emptiness," he said. "Emptiness, form."

"Is that a quote from something?" I said.

"I think it's a Buddhist thing," he said, "but I'm not sure. I'm an atheist, myself."

41 🐗 Grace Kowalski

5 FEBRUARY 2004. Irv's dead. What do I do now? Just the other night he said he loved me but even then I didn't know what he was to me. Now that he's gone there's an Irv-shaped empty space that's bigger than he was.

And while mourning him and missing him I'm really pissed off at him because it was his thing for Justine that started all this. How fucking old does a man have to be before he stops being an adolescent? There were four of us involved in the Justine business. Now half of us are gone and Rose Harland's dead and there are two Justines out there.

Artie is Irv's only living relative and when Irv was in intensive care at St Eustace he told Artie that he wanted to be cremated in a cardboard coffin and his ashes scattered at sea. No funeral procession, no service of any kind, just him in a box to the crematorium. So those were the arrangements Artie made.

From Fulham the streets unrolled behind the hearse through the everydayness of the living; from South London to North London and Hoop Lane with Irv in his cardboard coffin. The day was cold and grey. At the crematorium our footsteps on the gravel had a funereal sound. Some buildings stand, some sit; Golders Green Crematorium abides. It abides in its red brick and the seniority of the bodies it has swallowed. The cloistered entrance to the chapel looked as if hymns should be coming out of it but Irv had said no music so there was none.

When we were inside the chapel and Irv was ready to roll Artie put on a yarmulke and said *Kaddish*: "*Yiskaddal ve'yizkaddash she'may rabboh. . .*" The words had the colors of strangeness and the strangeness was heightened by the guttural sound. It was as if Irv were all dressed up in Jewishness for his final disappearance. We watched the coffin slide through the doors. No music, just the hum of the mechanism. See you, Irv.

The next day we collected the ashes. When we got back to my place I threw out the plastic urn and put them in a biscuit tin.

"It might take me a couple of days to get the next part sorted," said Artie.

"Where at sea are we going to scatter the ashes?" I asked him.

"Knock John," he said.

"What's Knock John?"

Artie handed me a postcard. "It's a sandbank in the Thames Estuary," he said, "and that thing you're looking at is a derelict World War Two fort that was built there."

"I guess it must have meant something to him."

"Must have. I'll ring you up when I know more."

I pictured the Thames Estuary: gray water widening to the sea. The fort in the picture looked sad in the postcard sunlight, pale and faded, a gunless platform standing on two hollow legs that were the round towers where the crew had lived. It looked haunted. I imagined the creaking cries of gulls wheeling over it but there'd be nothing to eat so they probably wouldn't. I guess we all have oceans in our minds. Now Irv was all gone, all his days and years and the oceans in his mind.

And in the meantime there were two Justines out there and I'd probably have to deal with one of them pretty soon. The last I saw of J Two she was snoring away in a chair at my place but she woke up and saw Irv standing over her ready to knock her out of the park with my Louisville Slugger. She did a real vampire snarl, sent us both sprawling, and was gone. We were bound to meet again one way or another. I thought I'd go looking for her before she came looking for me.

I picked up the Louisville Slugger and took a good grip. It was made of ash, thirty-three inches long, and it was thirty-four ounces of eraser. I could feel the power of it coursing up my arms. I didn't want to be seen cruising the streets with a baseball bat so I wrapped it in brown paper with one end left open for a quick draw. It wouldn't quite pass for a french bread but it would have to do. I thought I might have a look-in at Gaby's Deli and thereabouts. At first I was pretty scared thinking of what would happen when we met but then it came to me that I was just as dangerous as the one I was hunting. Maybe more so.

The bat had been left behind a long time ago by an old boyfriend who was over here for a while, Jerry Benson. He went back to his wife in Poughkeepsie eventually. We used to play softball on Sundays in Hyde Park with some of the Americans he knew. "You're a sucker for those high outside pitches," he told me. "If you have to reach for the ball you probably won't get any wood on it and even if you connect you won't have enough power in your swing." OK, Jerry, I thought, I'll tell her to come at me right over the plate and not too high.

I went slowly down Berwick to Broadwick, pausing every now and then to look around the way they do in cop films. This was a Thursday night, fairly quiet with a little rain. The Blue Posts looked warm and welcoming, a safe haven from the cares of the world. Certainly a peaceful pint in there would be a lot nicer than walking around with a baseball bat. I can't even remember the last time I was in a pub; I feel more lonely in cosy surroundings, I'm more comfortable drinking alone.

As I headed east on Broadwick towards Wardour Street I had one of those moments when I don't know who or what I am, don't know what's looking out through my eyeholes. I stopped under a street lamp and took my bit of *The Heart Sutra* out of my shirt pocket. " 'Here, O Sariputra,' " I read,

Form is emptiness and the very emptiness is form;
emptiness does not differ from form, form does not differ from emptiness; whatever is form, that is emptiness,
whatever is emptiness, that is form, the same is true of
feelings, perceptions, impulses and consciousness.

"OK?" I said to myself. "Are we straight now?"

"Doesn't matter," I answered. "Straight is crooked and the
very crookedness is straight. Let's just get it done."

"I have a thing for older women," said some drunk who
came weaving towards me.

"And I have a thing for creeps," I said, easing the bat half-
way out of its brown paper. He disappeared.

Very lively night in Wardour Street, lots of people, flashing blue lights, and two fire engines outside the Pizzeria Bar.
Past The Intrepid Fox and its rock music, a batwinged gar-
goyle over the door but not enough rain to make water come
out of its mouth.

Down Wardour Street to Old Compton with its melan-
choly gaiety and The Admiral Duncan where some anti-gay
planted a nail bomb a while back. Play 2 Win with nobody
looking like a winner. Lion City and Lesbian & Gay Accom-
modation Outlet. Now that Old Compton Street is famous as
a gay center I think it's become more of a tourist trap than
anything else. Bugbug pedicabs cruising for business. Form and
emptiness and Grace Kowalski with a baseball bat. *Mamma
Mia!* still playing at the Prince Edward.

Charing Cross Road then and Cambridge Circus, the Palace
Theatre and *Les Misérables*. By now I wasn't paying much
attention to what I passed and what passed me. I could feel
myself getting closer to what was waiting for me, and Charing Cross Road with all its lights and colors became a long
darkness where the Leicester Square tube station appeared
after a while, then Wyndhams where *Dinner* was flaunting its

reviews. I'd intended to look in at Gaby's Deli but something was pulling me towards Cecil Court so I went with it and turned left at Café Uno. The paving was glistening under the lamps and the darkness funneled me forward.

There she was, leaning against the Watkins window and crying. "You don't know," she said, "you just don't know."

I was close enough to smell her toad breath. "That's how it is," I said, "I'm sorry." When she saw me take the bat out of the brown paper she came at me right over the plate and I took a really good swing. THWOCK! Her head flew off across the court and a jet of blood shot up from her neck. I heard the head bounce off the building opposite as the body went to black-and-white, then flattened out, then vanished with a little sound like the ghost of a belch. I looked for the head but that was gone too. No blood anywhere on the ground. Nothing at all left of J Two. "That's all she wrote," I said, and walked home in the rain.

42 🐸 Artie Nussbaum

6 FEBRUARY 2004. A Google search came up with an outfit called BayBlast that operates in the Thames Estuary. They have a 6-metre Valiant DR600, that's a rigid inflatable boat with a 150hp Mercury Optimax engine. We can get a train to Whistable where they'll pick us up, take us out to Knock John, and have us back in two hours, weather permitting. That should give Irv an exciting ride before he gets scattered.

43 🐀 Detective Inspector Hunter

6 FEBRUARY 2004. Rachael Darling. I still think of her as Rose Harland. I haven't dreamt about her for a while; maybe she's at peace although I'm not.

No new bloodless corpses. Still two Justines out there and no leads whatever. Where did they come from? Goodman and Kowalski said I wouldn't believe their story and of course I didn't. I can suspend a fair amount of disbelief but I draw the line at vampires made out of magnetized particles. Whoever and wherever they are, they can run and they can hide but sooner or later I'll catch up with them.

44 🐸 Grace Kowalski

8 FEBRUARY 2004 Artie rang me up and told me about his plans for scattering the ashes but I said let's not scatter Irv in the winter when it's all cold and gray and raining, let's do it in the spring or maybe summer. Irv won't mind waiting a little.

I've got him on a shelf in my studio. Sometimes I hold the biscuit tin in my lap and have a drink while I talk to him. "What's a month or two between friends?" I say. "This is Grace talking to you, Irv. Linger awhile, OK?"

ACKNOWLEDGMENTS

I am grateful to the persons listed below whose good will and cooperation helped me with this story.

The behavior of Detective Inspector Hunter and other members of the police in this novel is mostly non-regulation. The same applies to the medical examiner, his assistant, and the mortuary technician. In order to ground the extravagances of my fiction in fact I was allowed, through the courtesy of Superintendent Heather Valentine, to visit Hammersmith police station where Inspector Steve Tysoe kindly showed me around and explained custodial procedure. Anthony Berry of Scotland Yard very patiently helped me with police terminology and organizational detail.

Mortuary technician David Webber was my guide at the Chelsea & Westminster Hospital mortuary.

Irean Pazook, of Regent Palace Hotel Reception, and Eden Parvus, Security Manager, gave me access to the room where the fictional Ralph Darling stayed.

Carol Lee gave me jewelry-making details.

Brom Hoban instructed me in the process by which Istvan Fallok isolated the video image of Justine Trimble.

Jake Hoban accompanied me on Grace Kowalski's walk through Soho to the fateful confrontation in Cecil Court.

Gundula Hoban, as always, helped me with all kinds of London detail.

Katherine Greenwood rescued me from a multitude of errors and put in hours well beyond the call of duty.

I find it impossible to stop writing, and I hope that Liz Calder, my publisher, may be forgiven for supporting my addiction.